Abby,

By Lisa A. McCombs

D1059589

Published by:

FriesenPress

Suite 300 – 852 Fort Street

Victoria, BC, Canada V8W 1H8

www.friesenpress.com

Distributed to the trade by The Ingram Book Company

Thank you Mom, Aunt Katie, Boone, and Rachel, for all of your patience, love and encouragement.

Thanks to the entire 2011 8th grade class at MMS for your enthusiasm and creative support.

Most especially, thanks to all of my former teachers and classmates at Monongah Junior High and Monongah High School. Those were the days...

August 23

Dear Abby,

My name is Abigail Van Buren Masterson. I discovered your name in our school library. My seventh grade English class is doing a newspaper activity and each of us was assigned a different section in the local newspaper. Mine is Section B and that's where I saw your advice column. At first I thought Miss Hendershot (my English teacher) was playing a joke on me and some how put my name in the newspaper as a silly prank for the "new kid", since that's what I am, the "new kid". But, then I realized that, no, I am actually named after someone famous and that's really cool. It's like Carmen (I mean, KARMA) and I plan to view that as a good sign for the beginning of my new school year, in a new school, in a new town. Any way, the assignment is to research something we read about in our assigned section of the newspaper. I found you, so, viola!, you are now my research topic!

I will be writing to you in this special diary that my mom let me buy when we shopped for school supplies last week after settling into the new apartment and getting my little brother, Joey, and I enrolled in school. He will be a first grader at Monongah

Elementary and I am a seventh grader at Monongah Junior High School. This will be my fifth school in seven years, but Momma says that we are now "home" and we won't need to roam around any more. I don't know why she feels this, but I plan to trust her intuition. It would be REALLY great to stay put. It's difficult making friends when you know that you'll probably never see them again.

Well, I just wanted to introduce myself and let you know that we will be spending A LOT of time together.

Sincerely,
Abigail Van Buren Masterson

P.S. I like that your job is to give folks advice. I might need some this year.

August 25

Dear Abby,

Because it's the weekend I cannot go to the school library to read your column in the newspaper, but Momma said she would bring a copy home from her job at the diner. She didn't have any problems getting a job here. In fact, I think she had already arranged to work at Monti's Diner before we even got here. And she seems to know the owner pretty well, which is strange since I have never heard of this town and she has never mentioned knowing ANYone ANYwhere. I think I would remember a place with such a weird name. Mo-non-gah. Maybe we moved to another dimension?

Anyway, she said she would bring home a paper and leftovers of the daily lunch special for dinner if I would keep an eye on Joey and make sure he doesn't wander out on to the balcony that is outside our bedroom window. Yep, I have to share a bedroom with a six year old, but Mom says it's temporary until we can clean up the other spare room in our apartment. I can live with the arrangements for a while if the pay off is getting my very own room. We have always shared a room (and a bed), but Mom says it's time for me to have "my own space".

And today I DO need some space to think. Joey is playing hide-n-seek with his imaginary kangaroo friend (yep, that's weird, but a friend is a friend, right?), so I'll just tell you what's on my mind.

After school yesterday I picked up the mail and (accidentally...the envelope wasn't completely sealed) read a letter to my Mom from a doctor in a nearby town. The letter was a confirmation for an appointment next week to discuss the results of a test she recently had. I don't remember my mother recently having a doctor's appointment, let alone a "test", but I guess I don't have my eye on her 24/7. Anyway, I looked up some of the words from the letter in our dictionary but I think further research will be helpful when I get back to the school computer. The words are "multiple sclerosis" and "spinal tap". I can't pronounce that first one but it just doesn't sound real good. Do you know anything about what this means?

Dear Abby, since your job is to advise, tell me what I should do! Should I wait for Mom to tell me what's going on or should I just admit that I read her mail? I already ran a damp paper towel over the unglued section of the envelope flap so that now it is completely sealed and she won't even know that I tampered with it. I am sorry that I read it, but I hope my mom is okay.

Oops! The kangaroo must have found Joey. There's an awful lot of jumping (human) around going on in the living room. Gotta go!

Have a nice day!
Abigail Van Buren Masterson

August 27

Dear Abby,

Today was great! We have a new teacher (I guess she's new. At least that's what it sounds like, but I'm new also, so what do I know?). Miss Tortellini will teach French and only a select few students will be allowed to take the class. They will mostly be eighth graders, but Miss Hendershot said there is a possibility that seventh graders with exceptional English scores (what one language has to do with the other, I'm not sure), will be accepted. That would be so cool! I cannot imagine speaking another language or even living in another country. Are we all the same across the world and just living in a different language? Have you ever been to France? Is the sky the same there?

Miss Hendershot asked us if we would be uncomfortable in an eighth grade class. I don't think it would really matter to me since I am new and don't know any of the students any way. We will find out at the end of the week if any of us little seventh graders get to go to French class.

So far, Miss Hendershot is my favorite teacher, but I have always liked English class, especially diagramming sentences (I know, I know...weird, huh?) and reading really good books. I hope we do both this year.

West Virginia history is cool, too. Mr. Davis is kinda young and likes to tease us, but he also seems to know a lot about his subject.

I think math class will be my hardest. Mrs. Mullenax is really strict and acts like we should already know the stuff she's going over in class. Numbers really aren't my "thing", so I'm afraid (especially with all the moving around) that this is not going to be an easy subject for me. I'll try my best, though.

Abigail Van Buren Masterson

August 30

Dear Abby,

Wow and Viola!
I made it! I am officially a French student!
Miss Hendershot made the announcement as soon as English class started today. There are only two of us, me and Adam P. (I can't pronounce his last name), and she told us that we didn't have to take the class if we felt unsure. I said I ABSOLUTELY will sacrifice my music elective to be a seventh grade guinea pig (my words, not hers). I mean, I like music a lot, but Mom has taken time to make sure that I learn to read music and practice my piano every day. (In fact, our piano is the first piece of furniture she retrieved from storage when we got here.) So, I don't think I'll suffer any intellectual failure by not being in MJHS music class.

Adam didn't look quite as certain as I am about it all, but I guess the thought of rubbing elbows with the more "developed" eighth grade girls and popular boy jocks won him over. He seems like a nice guy, but he is obviously interested in "advancement" on the COOL LIST. He is evidently an aspiring basketball star and hoping to be the team captain next year. I hope he doesn't leave me in the "dust", though, as a fellow seventh grader.

I can't wait to tell Mom! She'll freak!

This has been some week, but I think that MJHS is a good place to be. And I think I'll be just fine here.

Sincerely,
Abigail Van Buren Masterson

September 1

Dear Abby,

Today was the first day of French class and my mind is still reeling. It is such a beautiful language, even if the French aren't necessarily on positive social terms with America.

Miss Tortellini seems like a really cool teacher. She's really young and this is only her first year as a teacher. She is actually Italian and has only lived in America for three years. She speaks with an Italian accent, which makes her French even more fun to listen to. I don't know whether her "French accent "is really French or if it is Italian/French.

Our first lesson is to learn the French alphabet, which we will actually sing like we learned our own alphabet years ago. I can't wait to practice. Maybe I'll teach Joey, too. How fun it would be if he and I could speak our own language! This is going to be so much fun!

Sincerement,
Mademoiselle Abigail Van Buren Masterson
Viva La France!

September 2

Dear Abby,

When I got home from school today I found a note from Mom telling me that she took Joey with her to a doctor's appointment. I made her talk to me about it, even though I did NOT admit to reading her mail. We had a mother/daughter heart-to-heart after Joey went to bed.

I guess she's had mysterious symptoms of something wrong for a while. She said that her fingers are sometimes numb and her balance is all whack-o. It evidently is worse when she gets hot and she also gets tired more easily than normal. Because we've moved around so much she never went to a doctor, but since we're "home" at last she looked up the name of a NE-ROE-LO-GIST(another new word) and made an appointment. She told me not to worry about her, that this is just another adventure in life and that we can turn this into a learning experience. She tells me that God doesn't throw us more than we can catch and I know better than to question God.

The test she had confirmed the existence of MS (that's SO much easier to remember than multiple sclerosis), so I guess I am glad she had it done. At least I was until I read about what a spinal tap really is! I cannot believe that MY mother, the woman who cannot put a band aide on a cut if she has to look at it, allowed some stranger to plunge a huge needle in her spine! And remove spinal fluid! And then she drove home by herself, she helped with homework, re-made supper(I didn't know you should boil the water BEFORE putting the macaroni in) and getting us all ready for another day...and DID NOT SAY A WORD! Every time I take my mom for granted and kind of write her off as just a "given" fixture in my life, she pops up and, viola!, she does something totally unexpected.

I hope I grow up to be as strong and brave as she is right now. I think I had better start reading cook books, too.

Thanks for being there for me, Dear Abby.

Sincerely,
Abigail Van Buren Masterson

September 3

Dear Abby,

Today I made the mistake of taking my journal to school with me and , unfortunately, found myself "doodling" in French class when Adam sat down beside me, and even though he didn't obviously look at my notebook, I couldn't let him see that his name was curlicued all over the page. No, Abby, I'm not "in love". I guess he's just on my mind because he's the only person who really talks to me. He is cute in a red-head freckly kind of way. He's just SO QUIET!

Anyway, I'm home now and not even Joey is looking over my shoulder. I am supposed to be studying for my first French test, but I just can't get Mom and MS off of my mind. The only treatment for MS is still pretty much in experimental stages, but there are three injections on the market to choose from. Avonex is a shot injected directly into the muscle and is administered once a week. There is another shot that is taken daily, and then there is Beta Seron, which is taken every other day. This is the one that Mom and her doctor decided on. This will not stop MS nor will it make it go away because there is no cure for MS; but it is, as all the medications, supposed to decrease the number of attacks (or exacerbations) that are caused by MS. Mom will begin her treatments next week and she will have to "self-inject". Can you imagine having to intentionally put a needle in yourself every other day? MY mother? Well, she did do the spinal tap thing, so this may or may not be a piece of cake. Before she starts "self-injecting", a nurse will visit to show her the proper way to do it and she will get an instructional video that I want to watch also. Do you think Joey should watch it, too? I am afraid the thought of so many needles will give him nightmares, but Mom says he's braver than his six years looks.

I kinda wish I had a friend to talk to about all of this, but writing to you really helps. I guess you're my one and only friend for now. Is that okay? What's it like to have a pesky 12 year old constantly picking your brain? Annoying?

I hope not.

Maybe you can help me study, though. Tomorrow will be my first attempt at singing my French alphabet, so here goes...

You friend,
Abigail Van Buren Masterson

September 4

Dear Abby,

Well, I only missed 2 on my French test, but I could have done better. It was a silly idea to sing to you since you couldn't truly hear a word (or letter) I said or sang. Not a real accurate way to study, huh? Did you know that the Alphabet Song is the same tune as "Twinkle, Twinkle, Little Star" and that that song is French? Things just kinda work full-circle, don't they?

But, I guess if I'm going to study with some one I need to concentrate on making a friend I can converse with face-to-face. That doesn't mean I will stop writing to you, though. I consider you my best friend and soul mate. How many other Abigail Van Burens can there be on the face of the earth? This reminds me... Miss Hendershot said that we need to find out five facts about our research topic by the end of next week. Guess I'll be digging into your personal life real soon. I thought this research assignment was going to be really difficult at first, but Mom said we would look into getting our own computer over the weekend. I keep getting the feeling that she's staking claim to this town and that we truly are "home".

Good night and sweet dreams,
Abigail Van Buren Masterson

September 6

Dear Abby,

Our little family is now officially members of the 21st century. After church (yep, we even found a church to attend and, wow and viola!, Mom knew A LOT of people there) today we took a scenic drive to Morgantown (where Mom's doctor is) and had dinner at Pizza Hut before picking out our first desk top computer at Circuit City. So, we went to church AND we bought a computer AND we moved our piano into our second floor apartment. Would you agree that these are three very good reasons to believe that Mo-non-gah holds some permanence in the scheme of things or am I just being hopeful?

In my 7 years of school, MJHS is my fifth school and I can only hope that the educational roller coaster stops here. Mom seems happy for the first time in a long time, even with her diagnosis of MS. She likes her job at the diner and evidently has known the owner for a long time. I have only met him once, but he feels familiar to me. I didn't know we had roots in this part of the state, but then again, I don't really know we had "roots".

I guess it's time to tell you a little more about my family. I don't remember my father. He died before Joey was born and my mother has taken care of us by herself since. I think she was in college when they got married, but between raising babies and then becoming a widow; her own education took a back seat. So, she just takes jobs to support us, no matter where it takes us. My earliest memories are of the southern part of West Virginia, living in Boone County, then Logan County. I don't know how Mom found out about this place we are now, but it is truly interstate miles from what we're used to.

Evidently this is a pretty famous geographical location in the coal mining industry. In 1907 the world's most devastating mine explosion killed over 300 men and boys, leaving hundreds of young wives and mothers (mostly non-English speaking) to fend for themselves. Many descendants of this tragedy still live in the area. Mr. Davis pointed out the site of this disaster from his classroom window. It's kinda creepy to look out of the second floor window at MJHS to gaze across the river where so many lives were lost. Makes our lives seem almost effortless in comparison.

But, anyway, I like it here and hope that we can become a true part of this community, even though I still can't pronounce (let alone spell) most of the family names here. Mom's boss' last name is Mas-car-a (I thought that was something you put on your eye lashes). Our French teacher is Miss Tortellini (a type of pasta?). Even Adam's name is confusing. I had to ask him to write it down. P e l l i g r i n n o.

He explained that there are a lot of Italian, Polish, Czech, and Turkish immigrants who settled here years ago to work in the coal mine. I don't know why this particular location attracted people from the other side of the world. Maybe we'll learn more about it in Mr. Davis's class. I'll ask him tomorrow if he's in a friendly mood. Sometimes he's kinda grouchy and a little scary.

Oh, well, I need to get my bath and check on Joey. Mom is lying down for a while and I promised her that I would hang out with Joey while she rested.

Wow and viola! This has been a LONG letter. Sorry to talk your eyes off! You probably actually have a social life, don't you?

Good night and au revoir (that's goodbye in French),
Abigail Van Buren Masterson

FRENCH WORDS I HAVE LEARNED SO FAR:
Au revoir = goodbye
comment allez-vous = how are you?
Bonjour = hello
je suis bien = I am well.
S'il vous plait = please
manger = eat
Merci = thank you
ami = friend
Comment vous appelez vous? = who are you?
J'aime appel Abigail. = My name is Abigail.

September 13

Dear Abby,

Mom announced that today is a Doo Dah Day, since it is Sunday and her day off from the diner. We have unplugged the telephone and turned off the television. We are not to complain, do hard labor or share any type of negative energy. There has been enough of that this week, what with the MS diagnosis and Joey's Tonka Truck issues. (He tried to ride down the stairs on the back of his giant tow truck, only to discover TOO late that, no matter how awesome they are, Tonka's do NOT have brakes or a steering wheel.) A run to the emergency room and 4 stitches later, he has retired his Tonka fleet in exchange for a philosophy camp with his kangaroo. While he and Mom hung out at the ER, I stayed home to clean up the bloody mess on the stairwell. That's me, the one who stays behind and cleans up the mess. Evidently Mom has not taken time to more thoroughly explain her situation to Joey because I spent some time yesterday trying to explain to him why Mom suddenly is unable to run and why her speech is kinda blurry. But that's all NEGATIVE and a true Doo Dah Day does NOT allow that. So...here we go.

My mom's Doo Dah Day is an event of Joy, nothing but Joy.

It's pouring the rain outside, which really adds to the fact that we are sequestered to our second floor apartment with a recipe for Rice Krispie Treats and a Monopoly Board Game. Joey won't last long on the Monopoly game (six year old attention span), but I know that Momma and I will play to the death.

I'll let you know the results, mon amigo (my friend),
Abigail Van Buren Masterson

P.S. Here are a few community family names that I am learning to pronounce as well as spell. Good luck translating!:)

Shelosky	Manzo	Vandetta
Zachignini	Paglario	Carvollani
Delovich	Pulice	Angelinni
Kelosky		

September 14

Dear Abby,

Wow and viola! I have a friend! A living, breathing gal pal! Her name is Patti and she is an eighth grader in my French class. She's really quiet, so I didn't notice her at first, but Adam was not in class on Monday, so Miss Tortellini partnered Patti with me for our class activity. We hit it off so well, that Miss Tortellini said we could stay together if that was okay with Adam (he agreed, but acted kinda funny about it) and Patti (she didn't have a partner since the class number is uneven and she agreed at first to work alone). I really like Adam as a French partner, but being with another girl just feels "bien." We've hung out all week at school. It's fun to have someone to eat lunch with. At first I thought it would be weird to have an eighth grade friend, but no one seems to care about the age difference. I guess because Patti is so quiet and I'm the new girl, we are both kind of invisible.

Fine with me.

Patti and I have decided to try to converse only in French when we are in public, so Saturday night she is going to spend the night and help me watch Joey while Mom works. After entertaining the "runt" until his bed time, we will practice our conversational French by learning some usable phrases. This should be a blast!

I will let you know how it all works out. I am just SO HAPPY, Dear Abby, to have a girl friend. I mean, I really like writing to you. You are so non-judgmental, and writing down my thoughts is always so "therapeutic". You will always be my special friend and (although you are my research project and I have neglected to research my five facts on our new computer) I promise that I will not stop writing to you. Right now, my social life seems to picking up, though, so I might only get to you once or twice a week for a while. Is that okay?

Vous ami,
Abigail Van Buren Masterson

September 21

Dear Abby,

Mon Dieu! This weekend was excellente!

Mom let Patti, Joey and I make Chef Boy-Ar-di Pizza Saturday night, and that just set the mood for Francois dining. (I know, I know, pizza is supposedly Italian, but the good Chef's name sounds kinda French). After supper and a double header of Old Maid before Joey's bath, Patti and I got down to the business at hand.

Only it turned out a little different than I expected.

Patti brought a couple of magazines with her that I have only seen from afar. Cosmopolitan and Marie Claire are NOT Mom-Approved publications and I'm not even certain she would be wild about me reading Seventeen Magazine, but there they were...all spread across my log cabin quilt, daring me to crack a cover. I didn't want Patti to think I was some ho-dunk (I am) pansy (Yep, without a doubt), but I really didn't want to look inside those pages, either. There was something definitely intimidating about the cover models smirking up at me. I felt like I needed to dress up a little before introducing my eyes to the no-doubt adult content of these chic volumes.

So...I stalled...and it worked. (I don't think Patti was that interested in the mags after all. I guess it's just an eighth grade stigma thing and one she is not enthusiastic about completing.)

We decided to make up our own Rock Star Names before reading about the "real" stars of rock and fashion. The way to find out your own Rock Star Name is to use the name of your first female pet as your own first name and use your mother's maiden name as your last name. This is the formula if you are female and for boys, they use the name of their first male pet.

I thought this sounded like fun until it dawned on me that the only pet I have ever owned was a pet store turtle and I have No idea what sex it was. How do you know with turtles? Besides, Joey named it Tutt because he couldn't yet say the word turtle and, wow and viola!, we didn't know if it was a boy or girl. So, need-less-to-say, my Rock Star Name just isn't all that exciting.

Tutt Mascara. That's me.

Oh, my gosh. Wow and viola! I cannot believe that I over looked the fact that my mother's maiden name is one of those funny, difficult- to -spell names that makes up the majority of people in our new home town! AND, it's the same name as her boss!!!!!!!!!!!!!! And the name of the diner!!!!!!!!!!!!!!

The diner! Wow and viola! Monti's (Mascara) Diner!

Is there a connection?

I don't think I can write any more right now, Abby. My brain is a little fuzzy and full of questions. I will talk to you later.

Sincerely,
Abigail "Tutt" Van Buren Masterson

September 23

Dear Abby,

Well, when it rains, it sure enough pours.

Last week was an awesome week that brought me my first girlfriend and now, after I told Mom about my Rock Star Name (without asking about her maiden name JUST YET), she waltzed in after work today with my FIRST EVER REAL LIVE CAT. I told you about the little pet store turtle. That was an easy pet for such a mobile family, even if it wasn't fuzzy, cuddly and fun to walk. (Too bad Tutt ended up the victim of a rather wide, furnace floor vent.) Anyway, a pet means permanence, and that's something we've never had much of.

So, when Mom giggled her way up the steps and into the apartment, struggling with a rather lively towel in her arms, I got the feeling that permanence was something that we might learn about and Mom's last name was no longer important.

"Matilda" is a five year old Seal Point Siamese with lovely blue eyes and an extremely LOUD speaking voice. She came right to me and purred her way onto my lap before immediately taking inventory of my personal hygiene by giving my face a good rub with her incredibly scratchy tongue.

At first she hissed at Joey (small person phobia or reluctance to converse with the male species?), but after putting him in his "place", she ignored his existence and continued manicuring my eyebrows.

I guess she has claimed me as her "person" and that's okay with me. I couldn't' quit thanking and hugging Mom, even when she told me that Matilda was a gift from her boss. The cat had belonged to his wife, but Mrs. Mascara just completed her second full year in a Nursing Home and he really didn't have time to spend with her pet. He told Mom that he felt his wife would want us to take care of her "Waltzing Matilda".

Mom seemed overly emotional about this sentiment, but I didn't ask any questions. I guess I was just too interested in moi (that's "me" in French) and the excitement of my new pet. I know that's not a very grown up or considerate attitude, but Mom didn't seem to mind. She has been acting a little strange lately. I guess I would, too, if I knew I had to start giving myself shots soon. The home nurse is supposed to visit one day next week to show Mom how to use her new "auto injector", which is a gadget that kinda pushes the needle plunger for you. That doesn't sound too awful, does it?

After I introduced Matilda to her new litter box and showed her where her food bowl would be I herded her into my bedroom where she promptly burrowed under my comforter and fell asleep.

I can't wait to tell Patti that my new Rock Star Name is Matilda! I think that's even a French name. Wow and viola! That is SO COOL and BIEN! I don't think I'll even add a last name. I'll be like Madonna or Beyonce or Cher or Prince and just stick with the one name.

Yours,
Matilda (a.k.a. Abigail Van Buren Masterson)

P.S. Joey has decided that Matilda is his own personal dress-up doll, but she's not in agreement. Before he went to bed tonight, he tried to put a pair of his pajamas on the cat. It wasn't a pleasant event. I'm glad that cat doesn't have claws!

September 25

Dear Abby,

I don't know where to begin. Just when I think life is smoothing out and getting good, the "merde" (yep, my first French curse word) hits the proverbial fan. When I asked Mom about her maiden name and the "coincidence" that I realized, she got very, very quiet and couldn't look me in the eye. After several minutes of uncomfortable silence, I grabbed Matilda and stomped off to my room. I know that wasn't a very adult reaction, but she just can't clam up like that, Abby, and refuse to talk to me. All I have ever known is Mom, me, and Joey. We depend on one another for every thing, including honesty. Why won't she talk to me, Abby? All my suspicions about this place must be real, but Mom won't tell me anything. I know now why I feel like people look at me strangely and why that little ol' lady in church patted my hand and nearly cried when she looked at me. WHAT IS GOING ON? Am I just being paranoid?

And speaking of church...why did we just "happen" into the one that we did? There are 3 churches in Monongah, all different denominations. Not being faithful church goers, how did Mom decide to take us to the one where everyone seemed to know her? Adam and his family were there. Mr. Mascara was there. A multitude of persons with unpronounceable names surrounded us at "meet and greet" time and EVERYONE seemed to know my mother.

I feel like there is just TOO much stuff happening in my life right now: the move to Monongah, a new school, French class, Mom's MS. I was real excited about being asked to join the church youth group, but with all those wistful (nice word, huh?) stares from the adults, I get the weird feeling that I'm joining some type of voodoo cult. It's like they know so much about me...stuff I don't even know.

Wow and viola, I am just exhausted thinking about it all.

I'm just glad we decided to put the new computer in my bed room, so at least I can work on my research until Mom decides that I have the right to know something about this whole situation. I'm just having trouble staying focused, though. I think I'll just curl up under the covers with Matilda for a while.

If you are on advice duty, Abby, I could use some about now.

Wanting to be mad, but definitely more scared than anything,
Abigail Van Buren Masterson

FACTS ABOUT DEAR ABBY
- born July 4 (cool) 1918
- has twin sister who also gave advice (Ann Landers)
- real name is Pauline Esther Friedman and twin sister's name is Esther Pauline Friedman (weird)
- grew up in Sioux City, Iowa
- twin sister is 17 minutes older than Dear Abby
- the name Abigail is Biblical and Van Buren was a U.S. president

September 26

Dear Abby,

Matilda sleeps with me every night. It's so funny. She wiggles her way all the way to the bottom of my bed (under the covers) and sleeps on my feet. The best thing about having such a devoted pet is that I can tell her everything that's on my mind. I know I pretty much do that with you, too, but I can talk to Matilda without picking up a pen or turning on the light. She's a very good listener.

Patti was excited for me and my new Rock Star Name and even wanted to know if I could come home with her after school on Friday for a sleep over at her house.

Mr. Moore, our principal, announced at school this week that MJHS will participate in the high school's annual homecoming events coming up at the end of the month, so Patti has volunteered us to work on the float decoration committee. I should be excited to be included, but Abby, I just cannot muster the enthusiasm. I think I am experiencing a mid-teenage life crisis, if there is such a thing. There is a heavy weight hanging around my neck and pulling down my very spirit (wow, that was rather poetic, don't you think?).

Speaking of poetic, I think I will go read my poetry homework. Emily Dickinson should perk me right up, right? I mean, most of her poems are only a few lines long, so they MUST be just silly, little light-hearted verses, right? I know I'll feel better soon.

Forlornly Yours,
Abigail Van Buren Masterson

Two hours later:

Boy, oh boy, was I ever wrong about Emily Dickinson. She's a REALLY depressed person!

Just listen to these few lines:

"Because I could not stop for Death –
He kindly stopped for me –"

...and that's just the first two lines! You can only imagine how "happy" the rest of the poem is!

If I keep reading her, I could become terminally depressed myself. Talk about "reverse psychology"! I have NOTHING to be depressed about after reading a few of her poems. Good night, Abby. I think things will all work out. I know that Miss Hendershot has reasons for assigning homework and for once this particular assignment really hit home. I'll have to thank her for introducing me to the most depressing person in the world.

Joey really likes poetry, but I DON'T think I'll be sharing Miss Dickinson with him.

September 27

Dear Abby,

I found a few things today and will put it all in a sequence of events for you.

Basically here's the story of my existence:

1. Mom and Dad fell in love in high school (Monongah High School)
2. They wanted to get married but my grandparents insisted on college first
3. They agreed to begin college, which they did, but "things happened" and I came into the world.
4. They married without parental blessing and moved away, disowned by Dad's parents and a disappointment to Mom's.
5. My father became a truck driver and was killed on the West Virginia Turnpike while driving home from a two week work assignment.
6. Mom's dad (you've already guessed, I'm sure) is Monti Mascara. He begged Mom to come home when my grand mother developed Alzheimer disease, but Mom was not ready to face the disapproval of her mother.
7. When Grandmother Mascara was put in the nursing home

two years ago, Mom's dad got persistent and Mom finally consented to give coming home a try.

Mom didn't want to tell me any of this until she "tried on" her home town. She just figured that she could treat this move as one of our many, but when my grandfather got a hold of her she realized that this is where we need to be. I'm glad. It feels weird, but right. She hasn't gone to visit her own mother at the nursing home yet, but I'm hoping that changes soon. Evidently it was my grandmother, not my grandfather, that totally lost it when Mom got pregnant with me. She pretty much told my mother to not "darken" her door if she chose to marry "that Masterson boy".

Wow and viola! Talk about soap opera city! This is better drama than anything I can find on TV. No wonder people stare at us. Mom and Dad must have been prime entertainment in this town at one time. Hopefully the drama won't spill over on to Joey and me. I am kind of embarrassed, but relieved to know some facts at last.

Mr. Mascara (I'm not quite ready to call him Grandpa) invited us all over to supper tomorrow night. I'm already uncomfortable, but willing to give it a try. It's just all so weird to have relatives all of the sudden.

Wonder if I have any long lost cousins floating around here? I don't even know if Mom has siblings. That's something she hasn't mentioned. This is huge, huge, and huge! I'll definitely get back to you later!

I have relatives! Are you one of them?
Abigail Van Buren Masterson

September 28

Dear Abby,

Mr. Mascara, oops, I mean Pap (Mom calls him Pop, so Pap just fit) has a lovely home. It is obvious that his wife was at one time a talented home maker. Everything is just so ...tasteful. It smells good, too.

There are photographs every where. Evidently Mom has two younger brothers who live out of state. She also has a sister who was at dinner with her husband and daughter. This is where life gets interesting.

I don't know why Mom didn't say anything last week when Patti came to visit. I should probably be mad at her for this, but I think I'm just a little numb. I definitely have mixed feelings about this. You're not going to believe this, but Patti is my cousin! Her mother and my mother are sisters! That definitely turned a possibly stressful event into a celebration, although Mom and Aunt Katie were kinda awkward around one another, but by the time we left they were hugging and laughing.

 Life is good or at least getting better.

Pap has a family portrait of him and his wife and their children over the mantle in the "sitting room" (he also has a living room, but the "sitting room" is the fancy room where Mrs. Mascara "received" company). My mother in the picture is absolutely breath taking, not that I don't think she is pretty now. She was actually the homecoming queen her senior year in high school. Aunt Katie told me that Mom and my dad, who was the quarterback and captain of the football team, was the most beautiful couple ever. Evidently Aunt Katie really liked my dad, too, which kinda created a rift between the two sisters at one time; but they seem like they are over it now.

I walked around the house for a long time looking at family photos until I finally found one of my parents together. Pap discovered me looking at it and I could tell that he was kinda sad even though he smiled at me when he asked if I would like to have that picture for my own room. I think this is THE BEST present I have ever received.

Pap invited Joey and me back any time and he seemed real happy to have his daughters and their families under his roof. Evidently his sons, my uncles, will be "home" for the homecoming festivities coming up soon, so we will have an official family reunion. Thank you, God, for throwing all of this stuff my way. I just hope I can keep catching all the good stuff and let the crumbs fall to the floor.

Happy and full of home made lasagna (Pap is a tres bien cook!),

Abigail Van Buren Masterson
P.S. Patti is my COUSIN! Can you believe that my first real friend is related to me? How cool is that?

September 30

Dear Abby,

Homecoming is certainly a BIG event in this town. Evidently the high school football team is of champion status and the entire community supports their efforts. The parade will consist of the team and coaches, the high school band and cheerleaders, the homecoming queen and homecoming court and the high school mascot. Every grade level has a float and our junior high has one to represent both seventh and eighth grades. The parade route is through town and across the river to the high school, where the festivities end with a huge bonfire and pep rally. It sounds absolutely awesome and with the crazy recent events in my life, I am so excited to be regarded part of the community. I feel like I truly "belong", so I am proud to serve on our float committee. Joey is even involved. He is going to be a lion cub on our float. Aunt Katie dug out an old costume for him to wear. He giggles every time he puts it on. (Matilda didn't particularly care for her turn in the costume, though.) Patti and I are trying to teach him to roar, but that just makes him (and us) giggle harder.

I am just amazed at the way the entire town is embracing the upcoming events of homecoming. It is as if the entire town of

Monongah is one big, happy family. Oh, Abby, I am so happy to be here. Mom is right. We are "home". When my uncles get here next week, we are going to have a barbecue at Pap's house and then we are all (except Mom) going to the nursing home to visit my grandmother, who I STILL haven't met (Mom is really being stubborn about that. I'm really sad that she doesn't even want to see her own mother, but I suppose that's just another part of this Monongah Mystery that has been unfolding).

We'll just take it all one day at time, huh?
Abigail Van Buren Masterson

October 1

Dear Abby,

The home nurse visited today while Joey and I were in school, so we didn't get to witness Mom's first attempt at sticking a needle into herself. We DID get to watch the instructional video, though, and I think it disturbed me much more than it did Joey. (In fact, he watched it two more times before going to bed and claimed it as his personal favorite video to replace the Shrek and Ice Age collection that he holds so dear. Wow and viola! Maybe he will become a doctor, a neurologist, and discover a cure for MS or some other neurological disease. That would be awesome, but of course he needs to complete the first grade before entertaining ideas of higher education.)

Anyway, the auto-injector is kinda cool. Mom just places a syringe full of her medicine into this gadget that automatically inserts the needle into her skin when she pushes the trigger. I guess that's okay, but she still has to convince herself to push the button that ignites the needle. She didn't seem too freaked out about it, though.

The nurse also left literature about a national MS Society that sponsors events and fund raisers to raise awareness of MS and to support the research of such diseases. There is a local chapter near here and Mom is thinking about attending a meeting. I hope (I think) she asks me to go with her.

After looking through some of the pamphlets that the nurse left here, I think I want to research MS a little more thoroughly. It is such a confusing disease and it affects every victim differently. Am I naïve (good word, and French too!) in thinking that 21st century doctors should have come up with a cure by now? But, then again, the common cold attacks nearly every American EVERY year, so I guess a little thing like MS, cancer, or heart disease is really a challenge, huh?

Wow and viola! It's just too much to think about on top of studying for a French vocabulary exam. Better get busy. I'm going to do it without your help this time. That didn't work out so well last time.

Bon nuit! (That's good night),
Abigail Van Buren Masterson

October 3

Dear Abby,

Working on the float committee has really helped me meet some more classmates and Adam has even "talked" to me and even "smiled". The theme of our float is Fighting Cub Pride (get it? Lion Pride?). So, it is all decorated in scarlet and black (Monongah school colors) crepe paper and Joey is not the only lion "cub" aboard. We have ten volunteers to dress as lion cubs and prowl around the float. The seventh and eighth grade cheerleaders will march beside the float, wearing their uniforms and waving their pompoms as they incite team spirit with their repertoire (French vocabulary!) of "Go, team, go" chants.

Patti and I decided NOT to volunteer to ride on the float (we decorated!) so that we can join the crowd in enjoying the parade. Adam, as part of the athletic program, has to ride one of the fire trucks that will be carrying the football team. He's not old enough to play high school football, but he is in training and considered part of the up and coming talent.

Big news, though, and I cannot believe that I waited this long to tell you. Adam asked me to be his official - unofficial "date" to the bonfire after the parade! "Official" because he wants us to be "exclusive" and "unofficial" because neither one of us is old enough to actually "date". Mom is real adamant about the "not until you are 16" rule of dating and I guess his parents are as well. It sounds kinda old fashioned after reading some of the Seventeen Magazine articles (yep, I finally relented, but Cosmo is still not in my immediate future), but I'm not too worried about it. The whole boy-girl thing isn't quite as interesting as watching America's Next Top Model with Tyra Banks, but there is something about hanging out with Adam that intrigues me. I just hope Patti doesn't get mad.

Anyway, the festivities are scheduled for Thursday night and the Homecoming game is Friday night. Mom has already agreed to take me and Joey. Pap is closing the diner early to attend as well. He must be expecting a big victory, though, because he has already made enough pizza dough to feed our neighborhood. We are going to meet back at the diner after the game for some gourmet Mascara Pizza! Adam is invited, too!

I probably won't have time to pick up pen and paper until after all of the festivities, but just know, Dear Abby, that you will be the first to hear all about my Big Homecoming in Monongah.

Bon soir, mon ami!
Abigail Van Buren Masterson

October 9

Dear Abby,

Miss Hendershot is giving us part of our class time every Friday to read "for pleasure". There was some rumbling from a few of the non-readers, but mostly the rest of us agreed that we are happy for the chance to read something not related to grades (and definitely NO MORE Emily Dickinson.) Joey brought home a poetry book yesterday and he has memorized three poems already. His favorite is by Shel Silverstein and he repeats it over and over.

"When the light turns green you go.
When the light turns red you stop.
But what do you do,
When the light turns blue,
With orange and lavender spots?"

I'm glad he's studying something more light hearted than we are.

Miss Hendershot has a really nice library in her classroom, with all the current popular authors. She even has the Twilight series! Vampire stories are really popular this year and Stephenie Meyer is a really good writer and the reigning queen of teenage vampire stories. I also like Sarah Dessen, but some of her stories are about things that I can't relate to. Not that I relate to vampires, but at least I KNOW they are just fiction (aren't they?).

I didn't read anything from the class library, though. I forgot to bring my copy of Dear Ann, Dear Abby (an unauthorized biography about you and your twin sister), so I decided to read one of Miss Hendershot's many magazines. She has a stack of magazines about MS, which I think is kinda weird. The one that I read today was mostly testimonials from MS victims and advice (for both victims and caregivers) on how to handle living with the disease. MS is such a mystery in the medical world. Every case is so very different.

The most interesting thing I read about, though, is all of the so-called "natural" remedies that exist for MS. Bee venom is supposed to slow the side effects of MS. Yeah, really! Like I would voluntarily allow a hive of bees to have their way with me!

Another crazy one is electricity. There was a case of a lady who actually grabbed an electric fence during a lightening storm in order to experience a "natural shock" that would cleanse her of the disease and "restore order to her brain".

Then there are the food supplements and they don't sound too terrible. Supposedly grape seed is a helpful addition to a diet, as well as green tea extract, pomegranate and acacia (whatever that is). While I read this article I made a mental note to make sure Mom takes her vitamin B and calcium supplements.

Of course exercise is REALLY important to help eliminate as much muscle "spasticity" as possible. As far as I can tell from what I read, Yoga seems to be a popular exercise choice for MS patients. Maybe Momma and I can take a Yoga class together. That sounds like fun. We can be "gurus".

Well, that's all for now. I hope your life is more exciting than mine is lately.

Sincerely,
Abigail Van Buren Masterson

October 12

Dear Abby,

Wow and Viola! What a weekend. The parade was SO MUCH FUN!!!!!!!!!!! And the bonfire was GREAT! There was so much positive energy flowing from the community in support of Monongah High School, the football team, and the coaches that we could not possibly loose our game.

And we didn't...Monongah Lions 47

Manfair High 13

This was my first ever live football game, but I knew enough about the rules by watching Monday Night football with Mom sometimes. (She's a big Dallas Cowboys fan for some reason.) We sat with Patti, Aunt Katie and Uncle Mike (Katie's husband), Pap, Uncle Jimmie and Uncle Steve (Mom's brothers), Adam and his rather vocal dad. Of course we were surrounded by old high school pals of Mom's because the entire town (young and some extremely old) seemed to be in attendance.

Pap's pizza was a big hit and we all hung out at the diner until nearly midnight. Joey fell asleep in one of the booths and Uncle Jimmie pretended like Joey was a football and carried him up the steps to our apartment under his arm until Joey started giggling uncontrollably. (Did I mention that FOOTBALL is BIG here?)

Adam walked me home and even looked kinda sad when I said goodnight. Weird, huh?

The excitement even carried over into church on Sunday. Pastor Smith (one of the few people around here with a "normal" name) led us in the singing of the MHS Alma Mater after the service. Football is a BIG THING in this town. Did I mention that?

Now we are back to a "normal" routine with nothing much to look forward to other than more homework and more French vocabulary words. Patti and I are going to resume our French "conversations" to improve our accents and "fluency". Miss Tortellini wasn't in school all week so our substitute teacher was kinda easy on us. (Not only did he not speak French with an Italian accent, he didn't speak English very well, either!)

I have done a little more research on you, though, mon ami. I still find it odd that you and your twin sister have pretty much the same name, just reversed (Esther Pauline and Pauline Esther), so I am not surprised to discover that you both had a nickname. Yours is Popo and your sister's name is Eppie. I do not know what reasoning is behind that, but there are so many similarities between you and your twin that a little difference is good, I think. Your sister is also an advice columnist, the famous Ann Landers! Maybe I should be researching the similarities between identical twins. No, I don't think so; but that would be a good topic for some other project. I'll have to remember that. Actually this research paper is not due for a grade until the end of the year. Miss Hendershot calls this a "long term" project. She said this gives us plenty of time to thoroughly "explore" our topic and to make "wise decisions" along the way. Adam said it also lets her off from grading it for a while. I don't know what is worse...being a student with nightly homework, or being a teacher who has to grade all that work.

Well, I had better get my things ready for school tomorrow. Patti and I are wearing a planned outfit of denim skirt, neon green tee shirt and brown sandals in celebration of the end of September. We figure we aren't breaking any fashion codes by dressing alike since the only time we are seen together is in French class and at lunch. Dressing alike will give me an idea of what it feels like to be a twin, so tomorrow I am living in your shoes, Abby.

Bon nuit,
Abigail Van Buren Masterson

A French conversation between Patti and me:

Abigail : Bonjour. Comment alle-vous? (Hello. How are you?)
Patti: Je suis bien. Comment vous appelez vous? (I am well. What is your name?)
Abigail: Je m'appelle Abigail. Enchante! (My name is Abigail. Nice to meet you.)
Patti: D'ou etes-vous? (Where are you from?)
Abigail : Je viens Monongah. (I am from Monongah.)
Patti: Au revoir. (Goodbye)
Abigail: A bientot. (See you later.)

I wonder when I will actually begin to THINK in French or does that ever happen?

October 13

Dear Abby,

When I woke up this morning my mother was not here. Pap and Uncle Jimmie were sitting at the kitchen table with their heads bowed over what appeared to be empty coffee cups. When I asked where my mom was, Pap's eyes filled with tears and Uncle Jimmie jumped up to give me a half-hug and pat me on the head. (I think he's as uncomfortable around me as I am around him.)

I guess Mom got up in the middle of the night to go to the bathroom and she fell when she stood up. She had no feeling in her right leg and she went straight to the ground. At first she just thought that her foot was asleep, so she sat on the floor rubbing the circulation back into it. After several minutes, nothing happened and she realized that she couldn't feel the right side of her face. She called Pap who in turn called Aunt Katie who then took Mom to the hospital. She's going to be okay, but she needs to stay there for a few days and will be treated with some type of steroids to help her overcome this "attack".

It's just not fair, Abby. She finally found out what her problem is and has been religiously giving herself shots. She's covered with bruises because of the needles and I know it has to hurt. She's even been trying some "gentle yoga" that we are learning from a book she got from the Book Mobile. She is having trouble with the exercise because some poses put pressure on her bladder and she has actually peed herself a couple times. (That's NOT something I want you to repeat. She cried when it happened and I felt so sorry for her. She says she sometimes can't help it.)

The point is, Abby, she's TRYING SO HARD to not let this disease ruin her life and her reward is going to the hospital for more embarrassment? Aunt Katie is staying with her right now and Pap said we would call after while to see if she's up for visitors. Joey and I are not going to school today. I'm glad. I don't think I could concentrate.

We are going to read more of Joey's Shel Silverstein poetry book. That should take our minds away from our worry. He's working on memorizing a poem about a guy who watches television so much he turns into one. I might have to change my mind about this poet. This may not be "Emily Dickinson morbid", but it's close.

Scared, scared, scared,
Abigail Van Buren Masterson

October 15

Dear Abby,

I finally got to see my mom today after THREE LONG days of wondering if she really is okay. She still looks like my mother, but kinda...small. Does that make sense? It's not that she lost weight or inches...she just looks...frail. I could tell that our visit made her happy, but I think it wore her out at the same time.

Joey wanted to stay and play with all the wires and beeping gadgets and I don't know if he was unhappy leaving all that stuff or leaving Mom. He doesn't like that she is not staying with us right now, but he seems a little bit less stressed about the whole thing. Everything to Joey is just one big adventure and I think that if allowed he would volunteer to camp out at the hospital just to be in the middle of all the drama there.

Uncle Jimmie and Uncle Mike try to keep him entertained, but Joey just looks at them sometimes like they are interesting aliens come to visit. They are funny. I just don't feel a whole lot like laughing these days.

Hopefully Mom can come home by the weekend.

I have learned some more NASTY FACTS about MS:

- Exposure to heat (hot baths or sunlight or hot tub) can quickly weaken a person with MS.
- Bright sunlight can also create foggy vision.
- Blindness or other severe vision problems often occur.
- Muscle and joint pain is common, especially in the legs and feet.
- Sometimes hands, feet or legs don't work well in the morning after getting out of bed.
- Stress (emotional and mental) can cause an attack.
- MS victims often stumble when they walk and loose their balance easily.
- There is no cure for MS, but it won't kill you. (A sign in the neurology ward kinda disturbed me until I started thinking about it. It said: I won't die because of MS, but I WILL die with it.)

Abby, I'm thinking about changing my research topic to multiple sclerosis, if Miss Hendershot will allow it. What do you think? It's not that I don't' want to know more about you, because I do. (In fact, the librarian at the public library found a copy of your book to teenagers called Dear Teenager. I haven't had time to read much of it, yet, but what I have read is surprisingly current considering the book was published in 1959!) I just think that it might be helpful to me and to Mom and even to Joey to learn more about MS since we're all going to be living with it. I'll let you know what I decide to do.

Your Friend,
Abigail Van Buren Masterson

October 17

Dear Abby,

I asked Miss Hendershot about changing my research topic and she said that would be fine, but that I still have plenty of time to think about it and to explore multiple topics. She's really intrigued with my journal to you and thinks that it could be an interesting creative writing assignment if I abandon you for MS. (That sounds totally strange.) She did tell me how sorry she is to hear about my mother, but she didn't mention anything about the collection of MS magazines she has. I thought that was kinda weird, but I didn't say anything. Maybe she just stocks up on second hand magazines for her classroom and doesn't even pay any attention to what they are. I read another one today, though, after finishing my seat assignment. Victims of MS should maintain a low fat diet, but that just sounds like common sense for ANYONE, don't you think?

I've been practicing my French accent for Matilda and I really think that her meows are sounding more French, too. Is that possible? Do dogs and cats bark and meow in their native accent?

Halloween is in two weeks and Joey wants to go Trick or Treating, so he and I are going to work on his costume tonight after dinner. He wants to be a hobo. I don't know where he got that idea, but it sounds easy enough to assemble. Patti and I want to dress up like French Mimes but we're afraid we can't pull it off without acting like clowns instead. We're going to have to work on our "serious" faces this week because I'm quite certain that Mimes DO NOT giggle.

Joey and I have never had store bought Halloween costumes and when Mom suggested it I was excited at first. Aunt Katie took us to Wal-Mart to look and I was SO disappointed at how "cheap" they looked. Mom has always made our costumes and making them is part of the fun. One year I was Alice in Wonderland. Mom made me a red apron with about a dozen pockets that I filled with props (a pocket watch and an oversized Queen of Hearts playing card) from the story. I loved my costume, but my classmates didn't "get it". That's the problem with non-readers.

I don't know how much Mom will be able to help us this year with our outfits, but I'm confident that Patti, Joey and I can handle a hobo and a couple of black and white Mimes. I mean, how difficult can it be?

Mom is moving around a lot better, but I promised to stay home and help cook supper in case she gets too tired. I actually make a pretty good burger these days, but she still helps me with the macaroni and cheese. Aunt Katie wants us to consider moving in with Pap, but Mom absolutely refuses to be treated as charity and wants to "take care of her own". Actually I don't understand why she's wasting money on rent when her own father is rattling around in that big house of his all alone. I guess there are more unresolved issues in her family than I have learned.

Well, little brother is ready for his first "fitting", so it's time for Mademoiselle Abigail Chanel to get busy designing.

Look out Project Runway!
Abigail Van Buren Masterson

October 18

Dear Abby,

Oh my gosh, oh my gosh, oh my gosh, Abby!!!!!!!!!!!!!!! When I walked in to French class today, there was a note on my desk with this sentence on it:

"Quels sont vos projets pour Halloween?"

Of course this is far beyond what we have learned so far, so I had to wait until lunch time to dig my French dictionary out of my locker in order to decipher the meaning. Patti denied knowing anything about the mysterious note and Adam refused to look my way the entire class period (I think the head cheerleader has his eye lately). This is obviously the work of a serous French student, because it is not one of those common phrases that you flip right to in a phrase book.

It's probably someone practicing their conversational French and wanting to know if I am dressing up for the Halloween dance.

I just don't know why the writer didn't sign the note. Actually, I probably should give it to Miss Tortellini. I bet she dropped it and it's just trash.

It was a good mystery for a few minutes, huh?

C'est la vie,

Abigail Van Buren Masterson

October 19

Dear Abby,

And the mystery continues!!!!!!!!!!!!!!! There was another note on my desk today. Once again Patti was clueless and I didn't even bother to ask Adam since he seems to turn red every time I talk to him. I thought we were friends, but I guess I've done something to tick him off.

This French message is definitely longer than the last one and I think I might have to ask for a professional translation. Since I don't know who is writing these notes, though, I don't know whether it is appropriate to ask the teacher for help. What if it's about her and some disgruntled student is just blowing off steam and thinks I'm fluent enough in French to share in a gossipy conversation? I think I'll just work on my own translation. It will be good practice.

International Super Sleuth,
Abigail Van Buren Masterson

Today's Note: Bonjour! Je ne parle pas bien le francais. VoudrieVoudriez-vous sortir la   discotheque avec moi? C'est s'amuser.

October 19

Dear Abby,

I didn't get a chance to spend much time on French translation last night and I'm falling behind since there was yet another note on my desk today.

Patti and I had to put the finishing touches on Joey's hobo suit and make some final decisions on our Mime uniforms. I think we're going to look sharp in our solid black leggings and the black and white striped long sleeve shirt patterns that Aunt Katie helped us cut out. We are using her sewing machine to put the shirts together. It's my first attempt at a power sewing machine, but Patti is a pretty good seamstress so I'm letting her do most of the detail stitching. I'm more in charge of our make up and I can't wait to paint our faces white!

Anyway, today's note was a little shorter and I get the feeling that the writer is waiting for a reply. I don't know how to answer, though, since there is still no signature and I don't know the question!

Here's my French note from today:

Parlez moi bientoto? Comprenez vous?

I hope to crack this foreign language code soon. I'm sure you're wondering why a mystery lover such as myself has let this mystery linger so long. Well, we can blame Mrs. Mullenax and pre-algebra. I've had math homework EVERY DAY and it isn't getting any easier. I have to go work on today's little bit of torture right now. Maybe if I can figure out math I can figure out who's writing these notes and what they want.

I promise to work on this soon,

Mathematically challenged,
Abigail Van Buren Masterson

October 20

Dear Abby,

Wow and viola! I think I figured out what the notes are about! I think they are actually love notes to Miss Tortellini and the sender is leaving the notes here at night (the janitor?) and they accidentally get put on my desk by mistake.

Why do I think this? Because I saw Miss Tortellini and Jack (the janitor) talking after school yesterday and they looked kind of "friendly". Oh, Abby, I hope you don't think I'm gossiping and I promise not to tell anyone what I saw (except maybe Patti), but I'm not sure it's real proper for a teacher and a janitor to hug. In broad daylight. On school grounds. Should I say anything to my mom? Or maybe even Mr. Moore?

Concerned, but determined to not be judgmental,
Abigail Van Buren Masterson

October 21

Dear Abby,

The note today was VERY short and I actually translated it right away.

Oui ou non?

Yes or no?

So, there is a question being asked, but I don't know what it is! I didn't know whether to take these to Miss Tortellini or not seeing as how they might be for her and Jack is pressuring her for an answer to something. My curiosity finally won over, though, and I left the notes on her desk today after class. I told her that I found them on the floor and I hope that my little lie will sufficiently cover up any knowledge that I might possibly have about her love life. I would really like to know what those notes said, but you know what happened to the curious cat. I'll just direct my energy to trying to put a straight hem on my Mime shirt.

Abigail Van Buren Masterson

October 22

Dear Abby,

Wow and viola! You won't believe what those notes were all about! Miss Tortellini called me to her desk after class today to give me a translation that was not meant for her at all, but for me. She said it appeared that I have a secret admirer and that SOMEONE is asking me to go to the Halloween dance with him. I can't imagine who would be asking ME out, but Miss Tortellini seems to have an idea about the identity of the writer. When I asked her what I should do, she said to think about my answer carefully tonight and then leave my answer (in French) on the floor beside my desk tomorrow. She said that would be a non -threatening way to reply to the mystery guy. Since he has never signed his notes, he obviously doesn't want to be embarrassed by a public reply.

There are only four boys in the French class and they are nice guys. They kinda hang out together (even Adam) like their own little French gang. Leaving my answer on the floor, though, will be easy for anyone to see (as long as no one picks it up as a mistaken piece of trash before it can be read by the right person).

Miss Tortellini just kept grinning at me while she helped me devise my plan. She kept mumbling something about amour, jeune amour. I just wonder if she, too, is facing amour (love) with Jack?

I have to remember that cat, don't I?
Abigail Van Buren Masterson

October 23

Dear Abby,

Wow and viola! As soon as Adam sat down in French class today he reached over and grabbed up my little slip of paper with my answer on it and tossed it in the trash can. I pretended to "accidentally" drop something in the trash can and retrieved the crumpled paper. While Adam wasn't paying any attention I "accidentally" let the paper float back to the floor between our rows. I don't know why Adam has become so tidy conscious, but the next thing I know the paper is gone again and he's headed to the trash can.

Not wanting to look totally lame, I didn't chase back to the trash can at the front of the room again. Instead I quickly scribbled my reply on a scrap of paper and shoved it off my desk before the bell rang to end class. I didn't know if the right person had seen my answer until Adam once again scooped up the offensive "litter", looked me right in the eye and said, "Okay, I got it. Geesh, Abigail, it doesn't take a rocket scientist to figure it out. What time do you want me to come to your house to walk you to the dance?"

Wow and viola, Abby! Adam has been avoiding me so much lately that I NEVER expected my note writer to be him! And he wants to take me to the dance! I wonder how he will feel about escorting a Mime?

Until later,
Abigail Van Buren Masterson

October 24

Dear Abby,

Well, I have truly been conflicted about my research topic since finding out about Mom's disease. I just figured I would continue to sneak into your life history and come up with an interesting biography for a grade. MS has changed everything...literally, figuratively, and academically. Because we are required to write a solid "thesis statement" for our paper, I have been playing around with some possibilities. I'm sorry, Abby, but I CANNOT create a point that I want to prove about you. I just wanted to talk about your life, but that is not necessarily what a "thesis statement" does.

The topic of multiple sclerosis offers me much more factual information on which to base an argument. In fact, I think I want to write from a personal point of view and discuss the difficulties that face not only the MS victim, but the family of that victim as well. When I talked to Miss Hendershot about it, she agreed that this would be a VERY interesting approach. I feel a lot more comfortable with what I am doing now, and I have to credit you with some of that. If I hadn't been writing to you I probably would not have figured this all out. Having a sounding board is really beneficial in a lot of ways.

Oh, by the way, Adam wants to dress up like a Mime for the Halloween dance, too. This should be a scream! It will also save us from being forced into "conversation anxiety" since Mimes do not talk.

Bonsoir,
Abigail Van Buren Masterson

October 25

Dear Abby,

Either we are really "good" at being Mimes or Adam, Patti and I are too ridiculous for words. We spent an hour this evening practicing our Mime motions first in front of a mirror and then with one another with Mom and Joey as our audience. They applauded enthusiastically and Mom said we were absolutely "extraordinaire!". She also laughed until I thought she would pee her pants (and not as a result of her recent difficulties). I haven't seen her so...animated in a long while. So, even if we did appear ridiculous, I don't care. I'm just happy to see her smile and to hear her laugh without having to (even if she DID manage to throw in that "I told you so" look when she saw me and Adam together).

This brings me to my next point, Abby. I have definitely decided to use Multiple Sclerosis as my research topic. I've been playing with my thesis statement and this is what I have come up with so far.

"The effects of Multiple Sclerosis spread further than the person that is victimized with the disease."

I know it's still a little vague, but Miss Hendershot said that as long as I know my direction for now that it will all work out and the right words will come to me. I just know that when I look at Joey's confused expression when Mom stumbles across the room or cries when she thinks no one is looking, or the sadness in Pap's eyes as he watches her struggle to hold on to a frying pan with both hands, or the frustration in Aunt Katie's voice when she tells Mom to take her time and let others help her, or the fear I feel when I realize that I am kind of the head of the household when Mom can't get out of bed in the mornings...I just know that doctors don't always see this side of the disease. For the most part, Mom does not visually appear handicapped or ill so, to the public, there is nothing wrong with her. People are just unaware of the difficulties that neurologically afflicted people undergo. That is the basis of my research paper. I hope I can do a good job of writing it. Mom, Aunt Katie and I are going to a MS Support Group meeting next week and that should be another good resource for my research. I hope it's not a depressing event.

Well, enough of that...I need to practice a few more Mime moves in my mirror reflection before going to bed. If we can keep from laughing at ourselves, I think Adam, Patti and I can pull this off and have fun doing it. It will be a lot easier once our faces are painted white. Mom says that when we're "hiding behind our stage make up" we should have an easier time of "getting into character". We'll see...

Good Night, Abby,
Abigail Van Buren Masterson

October 26

Dear Abby,

Our French vocabulary lesson this week is all about food and eating out. Patty and I agreed that this was really very silly since most of us rarely "dine out", but Miss Tortellini seems to think it's of import, so that, as they say, is that.

"Une table pour deux, s'il vous plait." (A table for two, please.)
"Nous sommes prets." (We are ready to order.)
"Je voudrais..."(I would like)

This is where Miss Tortellini gave us a list of foods in French and asked us to attempt translating in small groups. Talk about funny! I am glad that none of us had une fourchette (a fork) because we would have been poking each other with all the mistakes we made. I hope that one of our assignments is NOT to go to a restaurant and order in French. I can't imagine WHAT we would be served!!!!!

Bon appetite!
Abigail Van Buren Masterson

October 27

Dear Abby,

The MS Support Group meeting was very interesting last night. I went with Mom and Aunt Katie. We met the president, Linda, of the local chapter and several original members, as well as a couple of other newcomers who looked just as uncomfortable as we did. Everyone was smiling and cheerful, but it was definitely difficult to not notice the woman in a wheelchair whose husband fed her because she couldn't control the shaking of her hands. And the guy who walked with a cane had a pretty hard time of making his mouth form correctly around the words he said. My heart really ached for the young mother who couldn't hold her baby because she couldn't hold up her arms. Her best friend came with her and took care of the little girl and I could see the fear in her eyes for her friend. MS is such an UNFAIR disease!

I did enjoy the upbeat, positive atmosphere that was reinforced, though. Even when the conversation got a little depressing, Linda smiled and offered words of encouragement. We had cheese, crackers and veggies for refreshments after the guest speaker gave a talk about avoiding fatty foods and drinking lots of water. It's just common sense but I suppose these folks feel better thinking it's news "just for them".

Mom seemed to enjoy the meeting, but she and Aunt Katie kinda agreed that it wasn't really their "scene". For all the positive energy that Linda threw out there, no one really seemed to believe it. And that's definitely NOT Mom's "scene". Her "up" times definitely out weigh her "down" times; but, she said she'd give it another try if Aunt Katie was up for it next month. She doesn't like to judge too quickly and I think that's a lesson she's trying to teach me, so I'll go with her again if she wants me to. It gave us the chance to talk with other MS victims, so that's a plus.

Goodbye for now,
Abigail Van Buren Masterson

October 28

Dear Abby,

Parents/adults are so very unfair sometimes. I just don't think my mom was EVER a teenager. I mean, how can she get so out of shape about a little, silly think like a curse word? I just accidentally let the S word slip out and she went BALLISTIC! She has taken away my after school free time and phone privileges for the rest of the school week (thank goodness the Halloween Dance isn't until Saturday) which means I come straight home from school EVERY day and I cannot talk on the phone, so Patty and I better get all our "talk" out during the school day.

If I had been smart I would have cursed in French. I actually didn't mean to curse AT ALL. It just slipped out, but once it passed over my lips there was nothing that could be done to take it back. I was mad at first to be punished for something so silly, but I'm beginning to feel guiltier than anything else. Mom said I disappointed her with my use of unlady- like language. I don't want to disappoint my mom, even if she is being totally unfair.

So...no more foul language, even by mistake and DEFINITELY not in English.

Merde.

Merde!

Merde?

Merde, merde, merde.

Merde, Merde, Merde, Merde, Merde, Merde, Merde, Merde.

Merde. Merde. Merde. Merde. Merde. Merde. Merde. Merde.

Merde. Merde. Merde. Merde. Merde. Merde. Merde. Merde.

Merde. Merde. Merde. Merde. Merde. Merde. Merde. Merde.

Merde. Merde. Merde. Merde. Merde. Merde. Merde. Merde.

Merde. Merde. Merde. Merde. Merde. Merde. Merde. Merde.

Merde. Merde. Merde. Merde. Merde. Merde. Merde. Merde.

Merde. Merde. Merde. Merde. Merde. Merde. Merde. Merde.

Merde. Merde. Merde. Merde. Merde. Merde. Merde. Merde.

Merde. Merde. Merde. Merde. Merde. Merde. Merde. Merde.

Merde. Merde. Merde. Merde. Merde. Merde. Merde. Merde.

Merde. Merde. Merde. Merde. Merde. Merde. Merde. Merde.

Merde. Merde. Merde. Merde. Merde. Merde. Merde. Merde.

Merde. Merde. Merde. Merde. Merde. Merde. Merde. Merde.

Merde. Merde. Merde. Merde. Merde. Merde. Merde. Merde.

Merde. Merde. Merde. Merde. Merde. Merde. Merde. Merde.

Merde. Merde. Merde. Merde. Merde. Merde. Merde. Merde.

There. That should do it. I hope I got it out of my system.

Thanks, Abby, for letting me "vent". I promise I will not make it a practice to cuss at you in the future.

Sincerely,
Abigail Van Buren Masterson

October 30

Dear Abby,

Today Miss Tortellini surprised our French class with a free pen pal...from France! Each of us received a personal information packet about our new international friend. These pen pals are our age and gender and they all supposedly understand English...at least enough to correspond with us in our own language. Miss Tortellini is encouraging us, though, to write as much in French as we can because this is an opportunity for us to practice our French on authentic French speakers and for our French pen pals to practice their English.

My pen pal is named Lisette. According to her profile sheet she is 13 years old and has a 17 year old sister named Patrice. They live on Rue Montaigne (Rue means street, but the French put that before the name of the street) in Paris. They both attend ecole (that's school) and study ballet. (It just all sounds so...French!).

I am so excited about having a French friend, but I need to watch how I speak to Lisette. Miss Tortellini pulled me aside today to tell me that I have been using the word viola totally wrong. Viola is actually a stringed instrument and all this time

I have used it as an exclamation. She said I probably meant to use voila (pronounced totally different!) and that voila means behold or aha. I feel totally stupid, especially since you probably knew that already and have felt sorry for my stupidity all this time. Of course, being Dear Abby, you are too polite to criticize me. Thank you.

So, no more Wow and Viola! for me. I'll just have to find a new "signature phrase", as Miss Tortellini calls it. She's really nice not to make fun of me.

Speaking of Miss Tortellini, I am a little ashamed of imagining some kind of romance between her and Jack, the custodian. I should have realized that EVERYone knows EVERYone in a small town and that they are just friends. Evidently Jack had just shared some good news with Miss Tortellini when I saw her hug him.

It's none of my business anyway. Mom says she's proud of me for not getting "wrapped up" in the "drama" of gossip and hearsay. I didn't really know that this behavior is something that my age group expends energy on, but now that I know I will pay special attention to staying on the "straight and narrow".

Well, the BIG DANCE is tomorrow night and suddenly I'm a little nervous about the fact that I actually have a DATE. I was really excited when it was just me and Patti being silly mimes. Throwing Adam into the mix, not because we're all just friends but because he asked me to go exclusively with him, is kinda unnerving. I really don't know why that changed things. I hope it's just my mind being goofy and that our friendship won't suffer from this.

I just need to relax and quit thinking about it as a DATE, right?

I'm going to do that RIGHT NOW and go give Matilda an extra few minutes with her brush. That cat sure does like it when I brush her, as if she doesn't spend enough time grooming herself.

Between cat naps, licking herself and eating, her day certainly is full!

Off to bond with my furry pal,
Abigail Van Buren Masterson

October 31

Dear Abby,

Last night I dreamed that I was in Paris. At least I dreamed about Paris after I woke in the middle of the night from some crazy nightmare about zombie mimes crawling around on the street outside. It was REALLY weird and VERY disturbing. I woke up to find Matilda sitting on my chest and licking my nose (I guess that was her attempt to wake me up). Every time I closed my eyes after that I kept seeing zombies with white faces making "mirror hands" at each other while crawling around on the brick pavement of Main Street.

I finally realized that there was no way that I could cuddle up with Matilda to snooze away the last hours before time to get up. Instead I decided to start my first letter to Lisette. I know absolutely nothing about France and can only imagine the perfumed air and fancy ladies that float around in a cloud of fashion and romance. I would love to see the Eiffel Tower and to visit the Louvre. I really hope that Lisette and I can be friends and maybe even some day visit one another. That would be AWESOME!

I guess I drifted off some where after the first few sentences of my letter because the next thing I knew the alarm was ringing and Matilda was batting my glitter pen around the room and my cheek was spit-glued to my note pad. It's amazing how much noise a six pound cat can make! And even more curious how strong human saliva can be. I think I'll begin Lisette's letter again later. This one is kind of a mess.

This is going to be a LONG day. I hope I'm not too sleep-deprived to enjoy the dance tonight!

Talk to you later,
Abigail Van Buren Masterson

November 2

Dear Abby,

I don't know what happened. Adam wasn't in church yesterday and today he totally ignored me in school. I thought we had a really good time at the dance. I don't know what I could have done to make him mad.

Well, actually I might have an idea; but it was all a mistake, an awkward, unavoidable mistake.

Here's what happened...

Adam, Patti and I walked to the Town Hall for the dance on Saturday night. Our costumes were fantastic and we got a lot of attention with the mime gig, even if we did end up giggling way too much. It was fun. A whole bunch of us got out in the middle of the dance floor and did The Electric Slide and Miss Tortellini tried to teach us an old dance called The Hustle. Even though we all tried, it was just TOO funny and we did more laughing than dancing.

When the DJ played a slow song to let us all rest, Patti and I got tickled because Mr. Davis and Miss Tortellini actually got up and started slow dancing! Together! I didn't know that teachers did that sort of thing! That was shocking, but even more shocking was when Adam tapped me on the shoulder and ASKED ME if I WANTED TO DANCE!

I didn't know what to say. In fact, I couldn't say anything at that moment because my mouth was full of cookies and punch.

And that's when it happened. I got a little strangled on having so much in my mouth and trying to answer Adam and getting over the surprise that I....I guess I sucked that punch right down whatever sinus tube controls that whole traffic jam and before I knew it, bright orange punch flew out of my nose and right onto Adam's white, mime face paint.

Oh, Abby, I was mortified!

Everyone around us started laughing and, of course my reaction was to join in. Even though my throat and nose kinda stung from that citrus punch exploding so rudely from the wrong place, I knew that laughing was better than crying; but I guess Adam didn't see it that way. He disappeared off to the bathroom to clean up, I suppose. Patti and I didn't see him again that night. Head Cheerleader Sheila also disappeared after that, which was strange since it seemed that her job was to make certain that she had EVERYONE's attention at all times.

Abby, I was just SO SURPRISED. I mean, I know Adam asked me to be his date to the dance and I know that we kinda share a secret little "like", but I really thought we were good enough friends to not let something so ridiculous as fruit punch stand in the way of friendship. Wow and Viola!, I mean gosh darn, was I wrong! I just don't understand boys.

In fact, I just don't understand people in general. Yesterday Joey and I went with Mom to the grocery store after church and as we were walking to the car with our grocery cart that Joey just HAD to push all by himself, I heard a lady say loud enough for everyone around to hear, "Look at that woman! Drunk in the middle of the day and with her children with her!"

I didn't realize who she was talking about at first and had to look around to see for myself. When I saw the look on Mom's face, I knew that the woman was talking about her.

Sometimes Mom has a problem lifting her right foot. It's a condition called "dropped foot" and it is a direct result of MS. Instead of lifting her foot, she has to drag it beside or behind her, which causes her to stumble when she walks. She usually pushes the grocery cart when we shop because it helps her maintain her balance, but Joey really likes to help, so she sometimes lets him. That lady would not have noticed that Mom had a problem with her walking if she had been pushing the buggy but she had no right to make such an uninformed judgment. That just shows you what people are so ready to believe about others.

Just by looking at my mother, you really WOULDN'T know there was anything wrong with her, which just makes Multiple Sclerosis even more unfair. The public doesn't always see the inside story.

And now Adam is being kinda unfair to me because he doesn't know my inside story. I didn't mean to snort punch in his face, Abby. I really like Adam, maybe a little too much. I really did want to dance with him. I just didn't realize he wanted to dance with me! He caught me off guard. He's going to have to talk to me soon, though, because he's part of my conversational French group and we have a project due next week.

C'est la vie...what will be, will be,
Abigail Van Buren Masterson

November 7

Dear Abby,

I was right about Adam...he was forced to acknowledge me when Miss Tortellini took us all to the University for our French class project. She got us invited to the campus French club meeting where she expected us to speak in French as much as possible. There were actually only two authentic French natives there, but Francais was flowing every where. Our class stuck out like that ol' sore thumb. We all smiled A LOT and nodded our heads up and down like we knew what was going on. I did actually understand a word or two here and there, but by the time I realized that I understood, it was too late to correctly put together a response.

I think Miss Tortellini got a kick out of our obvious discomfort. I hate to say that because she truly is one of the nicest teachers I've ever known and she takes SO much time with her students that we know she's sincere; but I really think she was a little satisfied with our discomfort!

The French Club meeting lasted until noon. Miss Tortellini instructed our Field Trip bus driver to take us to Pizza Hut for lunch and that's where we got to eat and talk about our experience. It felt good to talk in English again. I think this might have been one of the points of this whole experience. We talk a lot about "diversity" and "tolerating differences" in school and how it feels to be in a minority. Well, we the French students of Monongah Junior High School, were definitely in the minority today!

I couldn't believe that Adam actually sat beside me at the restaurant and at first I didn't think he was going to say a word, but after most of the group chatter died down he nudged my elbow and said that he was sorry about ignoring me lately and he sincerely looked sorry, Abby. I don't think he really wanted to "rat them out", but he said that he was embarrassed by the rest of the football players who laughed about him being "spit" on by a seventh grader when he asked me to dance. He said he realized that they were not truly his friends and that he would rather hang out with me and Patti then those "jerks" from now on. I guess I'm just caught up in my own world of "niceness", Abby, because I don't understand how people (especially supposed pals) can make fun of something like that. They called him names and made fun of him because he couldn't even get a goofy little seventh grader to dance with him (even though he, too, is in the seventh grade) and that my reaction to his question was to barf on him instead.

I didn't know, Abby. I didn't know that he wasn't talking to me because of that peer pressure and shame his "friends" was inflicting on him. I like him too much to be a reason for his pain, Abby, and I am so relieved that he figured out that it's just not worth it to be a part of their little clique.

I think Patti figured out what we were talking about and bumped my foot under the table to get my attention. When I looked up she gave me a wink and a smile. Before we got up from the table to return to school, Adam gave my hand a squeeze. I've got good friends, Abby. I am so grateful.

Abigail Van Buren Masterson

November 9

Dear Abby,

Pap was at the apartment today when I got home from school. He and Mom were sitting at the kitchen table trying not to look like they were arguing, which they obviously were. After grabbing a cookie, I went off to my room on the pretense of doing homework when I really just wanted to eaves drop on their conversation. I kinda already knew what they were talking about because Pap is not giving up on Mom about moving into his house.

It really doesn't make sense for Mom to continue paying rent when we could move in with Pap. Mom isn't even working right now, so why pay rent when she could just move "home"? I know she received some compensation or life insurance money when my dad died, but I just can't imagine that it is enough to support us for many more years. We have NEVER lived like rich folks, but Mom has always made sure we had everything we needed. She's also always worked really hard where ever we lived.

I think it would awesome to move in with Pap and I know Joey would absolutely be the happiest kid alive if he could be proprietor of that awesome tree house in Pap's back yard. I guess Pap and the uncles built it years ago and did such a fine job that the craftsmanship has allowed it to grow with the tree it's in.

Mom just isn't budging right now, though, and I can't really say anything or she will know that I have overheard some of these "discussions". Once again I'm involved in a real life conflict. Joey doesn't know how truly lucky he is to not be affected by adult drama. He just smiles through life like he owns the world's biggest secret.

Speaking of Joey...you would never believe, Abby, what my little brother did the other day (after he pretended that Matilda needed a paper towel cast on two of her paws)! I had left my math book open to the evening's torture challenge and when I returned to it, Joey had figured out the solution! Of course he did it in stick figures rather than actual numerical language; but when I asked him to explain what he had done, it all made perfect sense!

Abby, I think my little brother is a mathematical genius! He may be the answer to all of my pre-algebra prayers! Of course he looks at me like I'm some kind of retard because I don't understand how to solve the "puzzle". Am I looking at math the wrong way, Abby? Is it just a puzzle and I'm taking it all too seriously?

Wow and...sorry, I nearly forgot...Gee, six year old Joey is now my personal hero and mathematical guru. I guess we all have our "niches" in life, no matter our age.

I feel the need to meditate on this newfound philosophy. So, I will now drop to the lotus position and...

Ommm.......

Abigail Van Buren Masterson

November 10

My new letter to Lisette

Dear Lisette,

My name is Abigail Van Buren (not to be confused with the famous American advice columnist) Masterson. I am in the seventh grade at a small, community junior high school. This is my first year as a French student and I am enjoying the language very much. My French teacher feels that this experience will be valuable not only in helping me learn more French, but also in making a new friend.

I have a six year old brother who is a gifted mathematician and enthusiastic collector of unusual rocks. I like to read and listen to music. I like mostly female recording artists like Sarah McLaughlin, Jewel and Alanis Morissette; but I also like some of the praise artists like Chris Tomlin, Jar of Clay and Mercy Me. Are there any famous French bands or artists that you enjoy?

Oh, gag! This is awful!!

Dear Abby,

I had to stop at this point in my letter writing, because it just all sounded so "forced". I don't understand why I'm having such a tough time writing to my pen pal, when I write to you all the time and it just all "flows" so easily. I guess I'll just try again later. It's not like this is an assignment or for a grade. Miss Tortellini just wants us to gain a new friend. Why is it so difficult? I should be accustomed to making new friends, what with all the moving my little family has done. Is it because I'm "settled" and have subconsciously given up making new friends? Gosh darn, the human brain is truly an interesting machine.

I'll try again after while,
Abigail Van Buren Masterson

November 13

Dear Abby,

Today Uncle Jimmie surprised the whole family with tickets to a West Virginia University football game. Even though I knew that all of Mom's family (including my dad) attended college, I didn't know they all went to the same one. Well, WVU is the family Alma Mater and Uncle Jimmie even played football there for one season.

Attending games used to be a BIG THING that even my grandmother did. So, when Uncle Jimmie showed up with tickets, a party atmosphere took over and the entire family piled into Pap's SUV loaded to the roof with coolers, blankets, and people.

I didn't know what to expect and was a bit concerned with Joey's lack of enthusiasm at spending his Saturday at a sporting event. Joey has never had much interest in physical activities. He's more interested in books and brain exercise than physical conditioning.

When we arrived in Morgantown, we didn't just go right to the game. Evidently attending a university football game is more than an actual sporting event. Everyone gathers around and visits at what is called a "tail gate" where football fans eat hotdogs, chicken wings, and other spicy foods, consume silly amounts of Budweiser, and pretend to expertly pass around a football.

After we made our trek to the actual football stadium, we had to nearly fight our way to our seats, which Uncle Jimmie was congratulated on several times by Pap, Mom and Aunt Katie. I guess sitting on the 45 yard line is a GOOD thing in football watching. Either that or the cooler full of beer that those four shared prior to the walk to the stadium put them all in a very agreeable mood.

Anyway, the game itself wasn't very exciting. WVU won by several points. It was everything else going on around us that I found interesting.

College football fans are a curious species. At any given time an entire section of people somewhere in the stands might jump up on their feet to begin or participate in something called "the wave". Every time our team gained a "first down" the crowd would feverishly engage in some kind of complicated "hand jive" that Patti and I never did get the hang of. And, wow and gosh darn (I'm still having a problem coming up with a new signature phrase), when WVU scored, the entire stadium erupted in nothing short of a PANDEMONIUM. I have never heard such noise. It was rather deafening.

I can't believe that Joey actually seemed to enjoy himself. He joined right in on all of the stadium games and couldn't wait for "the wave" to some around to us. His favorite part of the entire game, though, was the marching band. They are called "The Pride of West Virginia" and I can definitely understand why. There are over 500 members in the band, including 3 directors, 4 twirlers and about 2 dozen flag carriers. When the band "took" the field at half-time, the stands absolutely vibrated from the massive drum section. It was thunderous. It was heart stopping. It was the most magnificent thing I have ever heard. Joey stood with his little hands clamped to his mouth in delight. Mom and Aunt Katie actually had tears in their eyes and on their cheeks and I even saw Uncle Jimmie wipe at his eyes. "The Pride" is such an accurate nickname if this is an example of the emotion the band inspires in its fans.

All-in-all, it was a wonderful day. Even the weather cooperated by giving us an unseasonably warm November afternoon.

There was a little more "tailgating" after the game, mainly to dissect the victory and empty the already lightened beer coolers. On the way home Uncle Mike, who doesn't drink alcohol and is usually the "designated driver", drove us around the university campus to point out to Joey, Patti, and me some of the landmark buildings from Mom, Katie's, Uncle Jimmie's and my dad's youth. I learned a lot more about my family during this little drive.

Uncle Jimmie got his college degree in engineering and evidently has turned down several "high paying" jobs to remain as close to home as possible. He and Uncle Stephen took their engineering degrees on the road, and Uncle Stephen likes working away from home but Uncle Jimmie said that he hopes to be located back in his home town in the near future. It's kind of ironic, since Uncle Stephen is the one with the family and Uncle Jimmie is "free and single".

Aunt Katie got excited when we drove by her former sorority house, but Mom just sat quietly throughout the "tour". I guess she was thinking about the education she gave up to marry my dad and become a mother. I wonder if she regrets her decision.

Uncle Mike is my only uncle who did NOT get a college degree, even though he attended WVU for three semesters before deciding against his "useless" (as Pap describes it) major in English. When Uncle Mike and Aunt Katie decided to get married and start a family, he became a coal miner to support their lifestyle. Aunt Katie graduated with a teaching certification and actually taught sixth grade for a few years. Patti came into their lives and my aunt has been a stay-at-home mom ever since. Coal miners make very good money, so they haven't needed her second income.

Wow and Vienna sausages! Being an adult sounds so complicated. I guess Joey is not the only one living an easy life. It sounds like my own life is pretty easy as well; at least for a few more years, anyway.

I know Mom expects Joey and me to go to college some day and I guess we are future West Virginia University students if we are to follow in the family routine. I wonder what I will decide to do with my future. I've never really given it very serious thought and I suppose I should do that. I think I'll start a list of possible options.

I wouldn't mind being a...

1. teacher
2. nurse
3. writer
4. forest ranger
5. journalist
6. book store owner
7. international super star
8. life guard
9. chef
10. concert pianist

Looking at this list makes me realize that I have a lot to think about as far as careers are concerned. I'm not really very good at any of these things. I guess that's where college will help me.

I'll let you know what I come up with,
Abigail Van Buren Masterson

Dear Lisette,

My name is Abigail Van Buren Masterson. You may have heard of the famous American advice columnist named Dear Abby whose name is the same as mine without the Masterson at the end. We are not related, just good friends.

I am in the seventh grade and will turn 13 on my birthday.

I like to read and listen to music. My best friend and I practice our French every day, but I am not yet confident enough to try it out on an expert such as yourself.

I have a Siamese cat named Matilda and a little brother named Joey. He's in the first grade. My father died when I was very young, so my mother is a single parent.

Gag, gag and double GAG!!!!!!!!!!!!!!!!!!!!!!!!!!!!!

November 15

Dear Abby,

I'm still not comfortable talking to Lisette. Should I mention Mom's MS? Should I tell her that I've attended five schools in seven years? Do I need to tell her about the grandmother that my mother doesn't talk to? None of this paints a very pleasant picture of me or of Americans.

I think Miss Tortellini has placed more responsibility on her students than she intended. I don't think this is supposed to be so difficult. So, why is it?

Abigail Van Buren Masterson

February 2

(Happy Groundhog Day!!! And no, you don't want to know what Joey did to Matilda for THIS glorious occasion! Let's just say that I haven't seen her since EARLY this morning.)

Dear Abby,

I am so sorry that I haven't written in so very long. So much has happened between November and now!

The big news is that we moved in with Pap a week before Christmas. Even though Mom has said from the beginning of this latest moving adventure that we are "home", it took at lot of convincing for her to agree to REALLY go home. I am VERY happy. Monongah definitely has felt like "home", but moving in with Pap "sealed the deal".

How do I know?

Matilda couldn't wait to get out of her cat carrier and race through the familiar spaces of her former home when we officially moved in. She didn't leave one inch of the living room "un-sniffed". After rolling around on the sofa and tapping the television screen with her clawless paw, she practically skipped to the kitchen in search of the food bowl that once was (and miraculously still is) there. I think she even danced a little jig in her litter box. All this time I thought she was perfectly content in our little apartment, but I guess even animals know when they are truly "home".

Joey is ecstatic with his new bedroom. It's Uncle Jimmie's old room and there is still a closet of memorabilia that he and Joey are going to go through together before Mom helps Joey customize the room to his tastes.

I inherited Aunt Katie's old room and learned quickly that she must have been the tidy one of the bunch. I didn't have much to clean or clear out so it will be easy to put my own "signature" on it. I want a Flower Child motif (new word thanks to Miss Hendershot's English class). I was really surprised when Aunt Katie brought an old trunk down from the attic full of her own Flower Child décor. We are a lot more alike than I realized. Her old bed spread is a bit faded, but we found a really INTERESTING desk lamp and I know I will get some decorating ideas from her old college photograph album. This is really exciting! Not only are Joey and I acquiring our very own bedrooms in our very own grandfather's house, but we are learning more about our family as well. Yes, Abby, if this is what it means to be "home", we are here.

Mom's bedroom adventure has been much different, though. She had to be coerced before finally unlocking the door to her old bedroom (the only locked room in the house). And once she did she stood in the doorway for what seemed an eternity before walking in and closing the door behind her. Joey and I really wanted to see her room, but Aunt Katie told us to leave Mom alone for a while.

The "while" turned into hours and when Mom came out her eyes were red and swollen and she was a bit "sniffly", but she was okay.

We didn't get to see Mom's bedroom for a day or two, but when we did Pap's eyes got a little misty before he gave her a nod of approval and went back to watching the evening news on television. I don't know how much she changed things in there but I like that she has a framed photograph of the WHOLE family beside her bed. The picture was taken at the nursing home during Homecoming Week. We are all (minus Mom and Matilda) surrounding my grandmother's bed. Even though Grandmother is smiling in the photo, it is plain to see that she is totally confused with this gathering. It really doesn't matter, though, since the rest of us in the picture know that this is our family.

Right beside the family picture is a teeny, tiny framed likeness of Mom and Dad. So, he is not forgotten, just pushed into the background where he now exists.

Mom finally visited the nursing home. She said it was really hard to do since her own mother doesn't even know who she is. I secretly think Mom prefers this since she still feels guilty for how she hurt her mother so long ago. When Grandmother doesn't know her, she doesn't have to own up to all that old pain.

(I found a letter in our newspaper advice column that is SO similar to this situation that I made sure that it was face up on the kitchen table this morning. I don't know if Mom actually read it or not, but the paper was not on the table at lunch time. I know the advice given was not from you, but I think you'll appreciate it any way. I'll include the letter and the reply at the end of my letter to you.)

I go to the nursing home with Aunt Katie and Patti every Sunday after church and Grandmother is mostly clueless as to who I am. She did call me Elizabeth one time (my mother), but before anyone could get too teary –eyed, she corrected herself and called me James, which made everyone laugh instead.

Pap seems really happy to have a house full of people. Mom isn't real thrilled about the financial arrangement. Pap insists on her staying home and not worrying about a job, but Mom is adamant about taking care of her own. Evidently my father left her a fairly impressive insurance check upon his death and Mom has used the money wisely, so she's still "taking care of her own". I did see a college catalog on the kitchen table yesterday, so I know she's giving some thought to her future.

She's getting around very well lately and the MS doesn't seem to affect her too negatively. In fact, if you didn't know she had a disease, you would never know by watching her. Maybe she will get her college degree in some type of program to help people like her. In fact, that's something I've been thinking about myself lately.

I am so glad that we moved in before Christmas because this had to be THE VERY BEST CHRISTMAS ever!

EVERYBODY was here. Pap cooked and cooked. Aunt Katie, Mom and Joey decorated and decorated. Patti and Adam and I baked cookies and wrapped presents. I've never seen so many lights or so much sugar in one place. And the music....oh, Abby, my family is one musical bunch of people. I had no idea that my mother had such a singing voice, but when she and Katie and Pap put their lungs to work, it was as if the angels themselves came to visit. Evidently my grandmother used to sing too and they had an interesting quartet. With Katie at the piano, the three remaining Mascaras filled our new house with hymns and carols from Thanksgiving until New Year's Day. It was awesome!

On Christmas Eve Pap served spaghetti and "calamari", which is a traditional Italian holiday dish. I was okay with trying something new until I found out that calamari is actually squid. Of course, I found out too late and ended up with a mouth full when Uncle Mike told me what I was chewing. Adam jumped back real fast when he saw the look on my face. I guess he was trying to avoid being spit on again, this time by a mouthful of chunky octopus.

Joey was very excited about Santa's visit and not in the least concerned about the Jolly One finding him in his latest home; unlike me, who knows the identity of Father Christmas but doesn't mind keeping up the pretense. I thank God every day for our new circumstances and hope that He knows what He's doing. I don't think any of us could take the disappointment of having to move AGAIN.

Everyone seemed to get their wish for Christmas (except for Matilda who refused to wear the angel halo that Joey kept putting on her head), whether it was under the tree or on the ground outside. Mom always wishes for a white Christmas and she sure got one this year. The temperature was below freezing on December 23, our last day of school, and the snow started accumulating around noon on Christmas Eve. And it didn't stop. For days.

Two days after Christmas the snow was still coming down and piling up. It was absolutely awesome. Needless-to-say, our neighborhood held numerous sled riding parties and was decorated with a variety of snowmen and snowwomen. It was all so beautiful, Abby; but, I have to admit I was anxious to get back to school by the time the holiday officially ended. There was just too much food, too much noise, too much excitement, too many differences, too much adjustment, and not enough quiet time. Maybe that will be the payback to living with Pap: too much family.

Are we humans EVER totally happy with our lives? There's either not enough or too much.

Abigail Van Buren Masterson

ADVICE COLUMN

Dear Helpful Helen,

My mother has had Alzheimer for more than nine years and when it became impossible for me to care for her, I moved her to a nursing home where they take great care of her. When my mother was well I spent a great deal of time with her, but since she's been in the facility, I don't get there as much as I should and the last time I visited she didn't even know who I was. And she seemed very depressed.

She has many friends who visit and my sister goes as often as she can. I have decided that Mother doesn't know me any more and it doesn't matter if I visit. I would rather remember her as the laughing, fun-loving individual who raised me.

My sister feels that I should visit Mother weekly and doesn't seem to understand my feelings. Am I wrong in not wanting to go to the nursing home?

Depressed Daughter

Dear Daughter,

Please go see your mother. This isn't about what makes you comfortable. It's about showing respect for your mother and alleviating the stress that your sister and your mother's friends have taken on by being the only family members to visit. Mom deserves to be acknowledged and loved no matter what her current condition. You will still remember the happy times you had with her, but you will never have another opportunity to say goodbye.

Respectufully,
Helpful Helen

Feb. 8

Dear Abby,

I got a letter from Lisette!

After stressing over how to write to her first and open the lines of communication between Monongah, West Virginia, and Paris, France, I finally sent off a mediocre letter right before the Christmas break, and she has answered! She included a photograph of her and her older sister. They look so much alike it's weird, what with the three year age difference. They both have long, dark, dark hair and the most brilliant bluish-purple eyes I've ever seen.

Lisette told me, in flawless English, that she truly does not enjoy school and that she hoped that having a foreign pen pal will inspire her to develop a "fondness for academia". I thought this was kinda funny because her writing indicates that she is a pretty good student, at least by American standards. Maybe she's gifted and a bit bored? I know that I don't like having her decisions about education in my hands. She DOES like music, though, but hasn't heard of many of the music groups that I mentioned in my letter. She said that "praise music" is not very popular in Paris and that people feel that church-related songs should be strictly in the original "hymn" format and sung only in church.

She loves to swim and hopes to participate in the Olympics some day soon.

She rides horses on the weekends and practices her ballet EVERY day of the week. Her favorite food is pistachio ice cream and she has a secret ambition to go sky diving. She only reads when she has to and currently has three (unknown to one another) boyfriends.

Abby, I couldn't have gotten hooked up with anyone any more different than I am if I had tried to on purpose. I just don't know where Miss Tortellini found Lisette, but I've kinda lost my enthusiasm for writing to her now that we have nothing much in common.

My next letter will definitely be a challenge if I try to talk about her interests. She didn't even write one word in French. That was disappointing.

Until later,
Abigail Van Buren Masterson

February 11

Dear Abby,

Guess what? After a week of snow days, we went back to school long enough to visit all of our classes and receive a backpack full of homework, enough to last us a few days. It seems that the school water pipes froze and it is illegal to have school with no water. Because of the severity of our snowstorm (thirty-seven inches and still pouring) maintenance crews will not be able to remedy the situation for some time. So....we get to enjoy a late winter break.

Joey is overjoyed, as is Mom. Patti is going to sleep over tonight and tomorrow, so maybe we can try to get back into some kind of routine, even without class bells ruling our day. We haven't practiced our French in forever and evidently Lisette's letters are not going to be much help. I was really hoping to become more fluent in my new second language, so I'll just study more and practice with Patti. I know this is only my first year of trying to learn French but I seemed to learn English fairly quickly, so I'll just have to be patient, right?

Snowbound in Monongah,
Abigail Van Buren Masterson

P.S. I am kinda disappointed AND relieved because the snow has caused all school events to be cancelled, therefore there will no Valentine Dance. At least I will not have to anticipate ANOTHER disaster at my expense. I don't think dances will be BIG on my future social calendar.

February 22

Dear Abby,

Eleven days later and we finally got to go back to school. I was really anxious to get back to my academic career until I got to French class and Miss Tortellini told us to prepare an oral report on our pen pal experience. Evidently several people have managed to correspond with their new French amis and it is now our responsibility to "share".

Most everyone has heard from France and their new pals are quite compatible. Adam's "friend" is the same sports enthusiast as he is. Sherry Mason's pen pal sent her an Eiffel Tower key chain and Pamela Watson received a letter entirely in French (accompanied by an English translation).

When it was my turn to report, I tried to sound as upbeat as possible, but when I mentioned Lisette's multiple boyfriends, Head Cheerleader Sheila snickered that no wonder I wasn't real pleased with my pen pal since I couldn't possibly understand the life of an obviously popular girl. She and her "groupies" covered their mouths with their hands and "politely" laughed at my own misfortune. I overheard Sheila say to another cheerleader that this was just another reason why I did not fit into this class.

And then she WINKED at Adam like this was some kind of inside joke. He turned a couple shades of red and refused to look up at me for the rest of the class.

The nerve of that girl! I don't know what I ever did to her. In fact, I don't even think I've ever had a conversation with her.

Later I found out that Sheila hasn't received an answer yet from her pen pal. Patti said she's just jealous. Patti hasn't received an answer, but she doesn't have an attitude about it, so I just have to figure that Sheila has something else against me.

I hate being so stupid, but I just don't understand why people want to act so "superior" sometimes. If Sheila thinks that she and Lisette are so much alike, then she is welcome to her; but I know Miss Tortellini wouldn't agree with that arrangement. And I think I should give Lisette the benefit of the doubt. It's not my place to judge her. I just can't relate to her lifestyle. Then again, I've only exchanged one letter so far.

I'll give her another chance.

Adam has me confused, though. After French class, he, Patti and I always sit together in lunch, but today he ended up at the eighth grade table with a couple of other "jocks" and cheerleaders. Yep, Sheila was right there drooling all over him and making sure that I saw her.

I don't know, Abby, what her game is, but I DO know that Adam did NOT look happy. What is going on with him? I hope I get a chance to talk to him later.

Until then,
Abigail Van Buren Masterson

February 23

Dear Abby,

Well, well, well...it appears that little miss Head Cheerleader has a bit of a crush on Adam and that is why she has been trailing him every where he goes. Even though Adam made his choice of social groups a while ago, he isn't so stupid that he would intentionally commit social suicide by shunning Sheila and her "cool" friends. Besides, he's just too nice to be nasty like that. Mom says he's just too nice to say "no".

Yes, Abby, I resorted to some Mom Advice on this issue and I'm glad I did. We had a really good talk and thoroughly enjoyed a Mom/Daughter Day today. She said she felt that she had been neglecting me lately and wanted to have some girl time; so, Joey stayed with Pap and we took a drive to Morgantown to shop at the mall and eat at one of her favorite restaurants. It (the restaurant) is what Mom refers to as a real "dive" but one that serves the best authentic Mexican food in West Virginia. She said that she and my dad used to "hang out" here years ago. It was really difficult to see exactly what it looked like inside since the lighting was very, very dim; but the clientele seemed to be college students of the "beatnik" variety. Located down a back alley in a sparsely populated part of the city, I guess I'm glad that I couldn't really see my surroundings. The food was good, though, even if I couldn't see what color it was. Mom just laughed at me and told me to enjoy the university experience of fine dining. I'm not sure this is something that I'll place high on my list of "things to do". :)

It was a good day, though. We both got a new shirt at the mall and I found a complete collection of Emily Dickinson at the used book store. Even if she is terribly depressing, I like the way she can put so much emotion in just a few lines of poetry. Mom approved of my selection and made a couple of suggestions for future purchases.

By the time we got home, I could tell that Mom was getting tired, so while she went in her room to lie down before dinner, I gave Joey the book I bought him and told him about the weird restaurant that Mom took me to. He loved the Shel Silverstein poetry book that I picked out for him and commented that it was really weird that I bought two books of poetry. I hadn't thought about it, but maybe I should add "poet" to my list of possible careers. I might as well explore all of my options, right?

Well, I better check over my math homework for tomorrow and make sure I'm ready for a new school week. We are FINALLY getting back into a routine!

Friends Forever,
Abigail Van Buren Masterson

February 24

Dear Abby,

Merde!

I know, I know, I swore never to swear again, but you will NEVER believe in a MILLION YEARS what happened to me today!

When I got to school this morning I noticed signs posted all over the school announcing a new club, Teens Against Drunk Driving (TADD). On my locker I found my very own copy of one of the posters, but with a photograph of mom taped to the center with the words "or is it drunk walking" written on it. The picture was taken outside Pap's house and clearly showed my mother stumbling across the lawn.

I told you that Mom has something called a "dropped foot" and combined with the every day balance difficulties of MS, she isn't real steady on her feet. Whoever took the photo obviously didn't know this or didn't care. In fact, whoever was responsible for this was just down right MEAN.

I tore the picture off of my locker and stuffed it inside before anyone else could see it. I didn't have to wait too long before realizing that my efforts were a little late, though.

Head Cheerleader Sheila and her posse came up to me before first period, complete with sad eyes that dripped of false pity.

"It looks like we're starting this new club just in time, huh, Abigail? I had NO idea what you've been going through."

I thought for a minute she was going to put her arm around me. That would have been TOO much!

I wanted to explain what she thought she had seen in that photograph, but something stopped me. Head Cheerleader Sheila just didn't seem the sincere type and the way she was tsk-tsk-tsking her sympathy, I decided to keep my mouth shut and do my best to ignore the consoling attitude she was attempting to create.

You know, Abby, just when you think life is beginning to make sense and that you have a handle on how things should be, God throws you a curve ball and tells you to pay attention. Just yesterday I discovered what an awesome confidante my own mother could be, but there was NO WAY I could share this breaking news with her. It would hurt too much and I did NOT want to do anything that would hurt my mother more than she suffered already. I don't know if I can even talk to Patti about it, but I'm sure the rumor mill will circulate it back to her regardless.

Help me, Abby, please...
Abigail Van Buren Masterson

February 27

Dear Abby,

Yep, Patti heard all about my new little drama and she is convinced that Sheila is behind the whole rotten deal. In fact, Teens Against Drunk Driving was supposedly Sheila's idea, but Mr. Moore told her that he had no teacher available to sponsor the group and that it wasn't going to happen this year. She put the posters up anyway and was called into the office for a little "chat" with the principal before the posters disappeared.

I almost wish I could bask in the satisfaction of her being chastised for her actions, but I really just feel sorry for her. I want to be mad, so very mad, but I'm just sad instead. I'm sad that my mother and people like her have to tolerate such reactions to something they have no control over. Would it matter if Sheila knew the truth?

Miss Hendershot found me staring out the window after her class and I posed that very question to her (without mentioning Sheila's name, of course). She told me that people are just sometimes cruel for no reason. It often was a result of jealousy or immaturity or ignorance. I just can't figure out why Sheila is jealous of me. She's obviously the eighth grader, so she is obviously the mature one, right?

Miss Hendershot sat with me for several minutes before patting my hand and telling me that if I ever needed to talk I could come to her any time. I thought that was really very nice as well as kinda weird. Miss Hendershot is a really nice person, but she's so "private" and not at all smiley. She's never been married and doesn't have any kind of known social life (although, how do we know WHAT teachers do in their spare time?). There are rumors that she is a real life witch, that she has no electricity in her house and that she lives with 75 black cats. She never smells like a cat, so I don't think that's true, but she never really seems very happy. I think maybe she's just lonely. But, I'm not going to start making judgments about her since that is exactly what Head Cheerleader Sheila has done to me.

Just being with Miss Hendershot reminded me of my research project, though, and I think I had better get back to work on it. I'll focus on my paper and not on the Drama Team of MJHS.

Off to hit the books,
Abigail Van Buren Masterson

March 1

Dear Abby,

I've been thinking about Miss Hendershot an awful lot lately and I guess there was a very good reason. Today during Silent Reading I chose to look through another one of her MS publications (that research project still needs some info) and I think my decision was "meant to be". As I mentioned before, there is no address label on any of the magazines in the room, so I was never sure where she got them. Today that mystery, as well as another one I didn't know existed, was solved.

Not only do the magazines BELONG to Miss Hendershot, but there is evidently a very important reason WHY she subscribes to a publication ABOUT multiple sclerosis.

Miss Hendershot has MS! That's gotta be it!

When I picked up the latest MS magazine, a letter fell out that was addressed to Miss Laura Hendershot. (I would never have guessed her name as being Laura. It's such a feminine name and she's so...not-feminine. She reminds me of Miss Jane on the old Beverly Hillbillies show that Pap loves to watch on the Classic TV Channel.) Anyway, I was so shocked to see something personal in something left in her classroom and the pretty name intrigued me. Oh, Abby, I know I'm a terrible person for what I did, but I did it anyway. I read Miss Hendershot's letter. (Once a mail thief always a mail thief, I guess.)

The letter was from someone who obviously knows her fairly well. A long lost friend? An old school pal? A distant relative? A fellow teacher? I didn't learn the identity of the letter writer other than that her name is "Nora" and that she was evidently in bad health. "Laura" had just learned of "Nora's" diagnosis and wanted to offer her some encouraging words. "Laura" reassured "Nora" to think positive and not get "distracted with negative reports of MS treatments and complications". "Laura" urged "Nora" to attend support group meetings and to "listen to her body".

Wow and viola! I have a difficult time thinking about Miss Hendershot having or being a friend to someone. I know that's awful of me, Abby, but she is just so "distant" and non-emotional. I mean, I know she's a human being, and she's not a mean person, she just doesn't have much of a personality other than that of an English teacher. I mean, I don't even think she goes to the bathroom. I know she practically lives at the school and that her favorite reading material is student essays and maybe something by Jane Austin. Just the fact that she has a friend is kinda weird. And I would bet the ranch that "Nora" is also a teacher and that the highlight of their social life is annual teacher conventions that last all summer long.

Anyway, this definitely gives me something to think about. I didn't get to finish reading the magazine and I would normally ask to borrow it, but I didn't want to be responsible for that letter and I needed to get it back to its owner without her knowing that I had snooped.

When the bell rang to end class, I quickly returned the magazine to a pile stacked on the reading table at the back of the room and hurried out without even stopping to say goodbye.

Abby, this was an exhausting day and I just don't know what to think. Is it possible that multiple sclerosis is so prevalent (new vocabulary word) that there are two people in this town that have it?

I think I'll ask that question at the next MS Support Group meeting that Mom and I attend. Maybe I'll even find out something about Miss Hendershot and the mysterious "Nora".

Mentally and emotionally drained,
Abigail Van Buren Masterson

March 4

Dear Abby,

Well, Patti finally got a letter from her pen pal and, happily for her, they seem to be a perfect match. "Molly" is actually an American living in France because her father is in the Army and stationed there. I'm not sure that Molly counts as a French pen pal because of her nationality, but she has been totally educated over seas and speaks fluent French...with an accent, I'll bet. Anyway, Patti won't be writing to a foreign country for long because Molly's family is being transferred back to the United States in June, so the cost of postage will be cheaper. I think Patti is a little disappointed with that news, but she's excited that Molly sounds like she could be a good friend. Of course, I'm jealous. I don't see me and Lisette EVER being friends.

Mom and Aunt Katie and I are going to another Support meeting tonight and I plan to do some investigating, for the sake of my research project as well as learning more about the disease itself. I'm hoping someone will drop some scoop about Laura Hendershot. I haven't said anything to Mom about what I learned about my teacher and wish I could figure out some ingenious way to bring up her name during the meeting.

I'll let you know what I find out.

Super Sleuth on a Mission,
Abigail Van Buren Masterson

March 6

Dear Abby,

I'm a bit concerned about my mother. When we got to the Support Meeting last night, there was a note on the door that the meeting was cancelled and if anyone needs to "talk" they are welcome to call Linda, the president of the group. Evidently one of the oldest members of the group died today. That really shook Mom up, even if she didn't know the person who died. I think it is more that someone with MS, a disease that isn't supposed to be the cause of death, actually created a situation that DID cause death. She tried to act brave, but I saw how she wiped at her eyes when Aunt Katie linked arms with her when they walked back to the car.

In an attempt to lighten the mood, Aunt Katie drove us to Tastefully Delicious, a gourmet dessert bar, for cheese cake. Mom rarely eats dessert, but cheese cake is her secret weakness so I guess Aunt Katie figured this would cheer her up. Mom pretended really well, probably for my sake, but I don't think she enjoyed herself.

I don't like the way Mom reacted to the death of a complete stranger. I think I heard her crying in the middle of the night. She has been incredibly positive since finding out about her disease. She doesn't let it get her down and she just acts as if everything is normal. She knows she gets tired more easily than other people, but she doesn't make a big deal out of it. She even deals with her drop foot like it's nothing more than an inconvenience.

Head Cheerleader Sheila would have NO IDEA how to handle this situation. She has NO IDEA the amount of pride that my mother exhibits every day. But, now, it's like this death has made the whole ordeal more real.

I just hope she doesn't settle into some deep depression or become terribly paranoid like Emily Dickinson!

I think my new research topic will be:

MS: The destroyer of all that is positive in life.

I think maybe I'm beginning to realize why Emily Dickinson was such a morbidly depressed individual. Life just literally "sucks" sometimes.

Abigail Van Buren Masterson

March 7

Dear Abby,

Miss Hendershot was NOT in school today because SOMEONE DIED! Is this maybe a coincidence?

No time to contemplate...gotta tackle math homework...GAG!

X + y = mc?

Abigail Van Buren Masterson

March 9

Dear Abby,

Life just gets repeatedly stranger and stranger. Before we left for school this morning, Mom told Joey and me that we would be having company for supper tonight. I didn't think much of it until I walked in the kitchen and found Mom, Aunt Katie and MISS HENDERSHOT sitting around the table murmuring softly, holding hands, with their heads bowed. I was so taken off guard that I didn't realize that they were in the middle of a prayer until "Wow and viola!" flew out of my mouth.

They all looked at me in surprise, but the most surprised was Miss Hendershot. She looked like she had been caught with her hand in the proverbial cookie jar. I don't really know why. She was the one in MY kitchen with MY family!

Aunt Katie was the first one to recover. The way she jumped up from the table I thought I was in a world of trouble interrupting them, but she came right over and grabbed my hand to drag me over to stand beside my English teacher as if she was going to introduce me to a stranger.

"Abigail, I didn't realize that my good friend Laura was your teacher. I don't know why I didn't put two and two together.

Laura, this fine young lady is my very favorite niece and I hope she is behaving in your class."

Miss Hendershot looked from Aunt Katie to me and then to Mom and back to me again.

"I should be the one to apologize, Kate. I should have realized that Abigail was your niece. I knew that Elizabeth was your mother, Abigail, but I still did not put it all together in my mind." Miss Hendershot really did look flustered and the most "human" I had ever seen her look. She didn't look real comfortable, either. Well, she wasn't the ONLY one.

I mean, Miss Hendershot was in my house, PRAYING with my mother and my aunt. It didn't make any sense to me at all and I really didn't want to witness any more; so, when I excused myself to do my homework (On a Friday night? Yeah, right!) no one objected. Miss Hendershot stayed for dinner, but I told Mom I wasn't really hungry when she came to my room to get me and, surprisingly, she didn't argue. I called Patti to find out what she knew about all of this, but she was in bed with a stomach ache and couldn't help me at all, other than to tell me that her mother and Miss Hendershot had gone to college together and that they had been friends forever.

Why was I the last to know all of this? And why was she in my house praying with Mom and Aunt Katie? And why did Joey not find any of this weird? (He ate at the table with them and was thoroughly entertaining from what I could hear through my bedroom door. I could swear I even heard Miss Hendershot laughing. It was truly an alien sound.) And why was Pap so glad to see MY English teacher in his house and treat her like a long lost daughter?

I did go out to say goodbye when our guest left, but I still wasn't very comfortable with her being there. I'm glad I did, though. Mom gave Miss Hendershot a hug before she left and I overheard her say some soft words about being sorry for Miss

Hendershot's loss and I don't think I imagined hearing the name "Nora".

I really AM in the middle of a mystery now.

Good night,
Abigail Van Buren Masterson

March 10

Dear Abby,

I didn't have to say anything to Miss Hendershot about her unexpected visit to my house. She approached me at the end of class today and even kept me after for a little "chat".

Miss Hendershot's college room mate, Nora Myers, was diagnosed with multiple sclerosis right after college graduation. Her health was stable for several years before it began to deteriorate three years ago. At first her sight was affected. Then she began experiencing severe migraines and lost vision entirely for six months. During this time, Nora's husband decided being a caretaker for his wife was not his idea of "living" and he left her for "adventures elsewhere". Miss Hendershot stepped in at that point and insisted that Nora move in with her. Nora's sight returned, but her body just refused to cooperate with daily functioning. She lost control of her bladder and had to be "catherized" (that's when you actually have a tube attached to a baggy type device that holds your exiting body fluids); all the muscles in her legs stopped supporting her and she was confined to a wheelchair; many days she had little to no sensation in her hands and could not even feed herself. Miss Hendershot became

Nora's sole care giver and house mate. All of those magazines in her classroom were hers, but not because she has a disease. She just wanted to keep updated on what her friend Nora was experiencing.

Multiple Sclerosis did NOT kill Nora. Miss Hendershot wanted to make that very clear to me because of my mother's situation. Nora was an extreme case who did not get medical treatment early in her diagnosis and probably succumbed more to the stress of having the disease than to normal progression of its effects.

Miss Hendershot told me that she never mentioned any of this to me because she knew about my mother and did not want to scare me with what she was living with as a caregiver. (This is the reason I never knew that she and Aunt Katie were so close. Miss Hendershot had NO free time what with teaching every day and rushing home to take care of Nora.) Every case of multiple sclerosis is very, very different and Miss Hendershot said that my mother is a remarkable example of what early treatment, exercise and mental contentment can do for a MS victim.

She apologized for surprising me last Friday and hoped that her presence in my family will not create a problem with our academic relationship. I told her that it would be weird seeing her in a social setting, but I would only be her student until the end of eighth grade, so I would try to be adult about the whole thing.

When I got to lunch later, Patti was sitting with Adam (surprise, surprise) and they were contemplating my "meeting" with Miss Hendershot. Once I assured them that I was NOT in any type of trouble, I looked Adam right in the eye and asked him what his problem was lately.

What he told me totally made me forget about Miss Hendershot and Nora and multiple sclerosis.

Head Cheerleader Sheila was definitely pursuing Adam's affections and had been following him every where and claiming to be his girl friend. Adam said that he had finally had ENOUGH and told Head Cheerleader Sheila that she could not possibly be his girlfriend because he already had a girlfriend…ME!

Can you believe it, Abby? He told Sheila that I, Abigail Van Buren Masterson, am his GIRLFRIEND! (If I want to be, that is.)

Wow and viola and voila!

I have a boyfriend! And it's Adam!

Stick THAT in your pom pom, Sheila, and shake it all around.

Forgive me for my sarcasm, Abby, but I just kinda feel justified. I can't wait to tell my mother!

Rah! Rah! Sis boom bah!
Abigail Van Buren Masterson

March 12

Dear Abby,

I feel that I need to apologize for my attitude in that last letter to you. I know it was a bit immature, even if no one else would ever know about it. I guess I have a conscience, right? So, in an attempt to ease my new found conscience, today I gave Head Cheerleader Sheila my French pen pal. I asked Miss Tortellini if it was okay. She was skeptical at first, but when I explained how different Lisette and I are and how Sheila seemed a better match for her, she relented and agreed to let me trade with Sheila.

I think Sheila was shocked with my random act of generosity at first, but when I refused to discuss it further, she agreed to write to Lisette as long as I didn't mention it to anyone else. I didn't understand why until I overheard her bragging to her friends about the awesome letter she received from her pen pal. What a phony! Why do people do that? Why does Sheila feel the need to pretend? Doesn't she realize that nobody actually CARES? And has she forgotten that I already told the class about Lisette? I guess phonies are also afflicted with selective memory disorder.

Oh, well, I feel better, though. I really didn't want Lisette to think that she got totally ripped off in the pen pal activity. I just knew that our relationship was NOT working out.

Joey received some fun news today also. Little league baseball sign ups are this week and Pap agreed to take Joey to sign up to play for Monongah. I am actually surprised that Joey is interested in playing a sport, but Pap is tres (French for very) excited. I think Pap worries about the lack of male influence in Joey's life and he feels responsible for contributing to that area of Joey's life. I hope that all works out for them both.

It doesn't feel completely right, though, to be thinking about baseball when there is still snow on the ground! I always think of baseball in conjunction with summer days! Just shows you what I know about sports!

Well, since I have a new French pen pal, I need to introduce myself and hope that we are more compatible than the last one.

Off to write the perfect letter,
Abigail Van Buren Masterson

March 13

Dear Abby,

I have discovered that one of the most challenging parts of writing a research paper is the actual mechanics of putting it together in proper format. My brain works faster than my fingers when I am typing, so I have to continuously stop to correct my mistakes. Mom told me to type the whole paper and then go back and make corrections. That sounded like logical advice at first, but I keep getting too distracted and have to make immediate corrections. Mom said that is a "compulsive behavior" and that I inherited that honestly from my dad, which means that it is NOT a bad thing to have as far as I'm concerned. I may not really remember him well, but knowing that I share one of his behaviors is kinda comforting.

Anyway, writing a research paper is easy compared to preparing it for publication. I had to change my font style, which also changed my pages numbers and page breaks, so I had to realign each and every page, ONE AT A TIME. Talk about time consuming!

Miss Hendershot has been extremely helpful with my final paper purpose. I feel kinda "funny" about that and do not want to publicize that information on the chance that classmates will think that I got extra attention since she's friends with my family. I do NOT want to be labeled a "brown noser" or "teacher's pet". She is just such a valuable resource, though, since she was a caregiver to Nora for so long. She has first hand information about living with MS.

I plan to ask Mom to read my final paper before turning it in. I don't think it will upset her and I really trust her opinion. I know I still have weeks before the paper is due, but I think getting an early start is a good idea...especially since the typing part is SO time consuming!

Well, Joey is waiting to "help" me with my math, so I had better take advantage of what time the "little genius" can spare.

Sincerely,
Abigail Van Buren Masterson

April 10

Dear Abby,

In two days I will officially be a teenager. I really do not know how I feel about this new phase in my life, but Patti seems to feel that it is a very exciting landmark event and has decided that we should celebrate in style.

Birthdays have always been rather personal for Joey and me. The special day is all about the birthday boy or girl. Mom lets me or Joey choose our birthday meal and then we have a scavenger hunt to find our gift. It's really cool and I had planned to invite Patti over to share my favorite meal of scrambled eggs and sausage, blueberry muffins, and cherry cheesecake. I kinda forgot that we now live in a proper home with a proper family, though, so what is normally a quiet event could turn into a real live party. This makes me kinda nervous, and I'm not real sure Mom is thrilled with the idea. Especially when she realized that we would be visiting Grandmother at the nursing home. Why, you ask? Because it is also her birthday, a fact that everyone neglected to tell me.

Yep, I was born on Grandmother Mascara's birthday. I was her very own birthday gift thirteen years ago. I was the gift that she refused to open and never acknowledged.

I don't hold a grudge about it, though, since I didn't know she existed.

So, as far as I'm concerned, I think we should just take the party to the nursing home. I can still have my quiet birthday at home; but Grandmother deserves the BIG party. Yes, thirteen is important, but she's going to be 65!!!!!!!!!!!!!!!!!

This will be a good reason for Mom to visit her mother. In fact, that is my birthday wish and since it is the gift I want and also MY birthday, how can Mom deny my wish?

Oh, Abby, I am a scheming little birthday girl, am I not?

Maybe this will be the very best birthday ever! Now, I need to think about what I can give Grandmother for her birthday besides putting a bow on my own mother's head.

Patti was right. We WILL celebrate in style.

Happy birthday to me, happy birthday to me, and happy birthday to Grandmother...happy birthday to us!

Nearly 13,
Abigail Van Buren Masterson

April 11

Dear Abby,

Well, Head Cheerleader Sheila is on the war path once again. She is SO annoying. Evidently she and Lisette are a PERFECT match and are fast becoming des amis meilleur (best friends). This she is positive about after only one letter exchange. I don't know if Lisette actually mentioned me to Sheila, but Sheila adamantly let everyone know that her pen pal had previously been linked with a rather immature seventh grader who KNEW NOTHING about real life.

Why does she act like that, Abby? She and Lisette were introduced BECAUSE of that "immature seventh grader". Sheila is such a jerk.

Patti got kind of huffy about the whole thing, but I decided to ignore her and just concentrate on my birthday plans. Mom is none too happy about my birthday wish, but I do not see how she can possibly weasel out of going to the nursing home, since that is all I asked for this year (much to Patti's disdain – I love new vocabulary words – since this is the BIG 13 and I should have my eye on something HUGE. Like what?).

Pap thinks my plan is wonderful, though, and is in complete support of taking the party to Grandmother. Aunt Katie is baking Grandmother's favorite angel food cake and we are going to decorate her room with green and pink streamers (her favorite colors). Patti and I are responsible for walking over to the florist to pick up two potted jonquils (Grandmother's favorite flower). Joey's job is to make sure that Mom doesn't disappear before time to leave for the nursing home. I think I'm more excited about surprising Grandmother than I am about it being my birthday as well. This is going to be great!

Abigail Van Buren Masterson

April 12

"Happy birthday to me, happy birthday to me!"

Dear Abby,

My birthday started out better than I could ever imagine. The mail arrived before Patti and I left for the florist and I was the happy recipient of MOST of it. I received a birthday card from Uncle Stephen, the March issue of Seventeen Magazine (a birthday subscription from Aunt Katie and Patti), and, hold on to your hat!, a letter from Lisette. That last was a TOTAL surprise. She did not mention Sheila AT ALL, but that could be due to a delay in mailing time.

This letter was much more interesting than the last one and I felt a momentary twinge of guilt for passing her on to Sheila. I still haven't written to my new pen pal, but I think I'll write back to Lisette first just to be polite. She actually mentioned the Harry Potter series and how she's really enjoying the books. For a "non-reader" I found this interesting and decided that there may be hope for her yet.

Grandmother was "blown away" with her birthday party. Mom tried to stay out of sight for most of the event, but her cover was blown when we sang Happy Birthday and Grandmother heard her voice. I don't know who was most shocked when she called for Elizabeth and suddenly Mom was in her arms, both of them sobbing like crazy. Aunt Katie later told me that those two hours were the most lucid her mother had been in two years.

I think we may have given Grandmother (and Mom) the best present we could imagine. We are anxious about how long Grandmother will remain "caught up" with this sudden memory spike.

Mom seems okay with her reunion with Grandmother and I hope that they resolved all of their "issues" for both their sakes. Mom hasn't mentioned the visit again, but I hope she agrees to go with me after church on Sunday.

After we returned home from the nursing home, there was more celebration (this time in honor of me), and it was exactly what I wanted. Quiet, simple, family...

I had my annual Scavenger Hunt (Mom writes silly rhyming clues and places them randomly around the house, eventually leading you to your gifts) after we ate scrambled eggs, sausage, blueberry muffins, and cherry cheesecake. Joey helped me solve the clues that lead to this year's hiding place under my own bed.

There I found a complete scrapbooking kit and a new digital camera! (And Matilda wearing a pink ribbon tied in a bow around her tail. I guess that was my gift from Joey. Poor Matilda!) What a fun gift. Both Patti and I will enjoy this. But I didn't wait for Patti to see it before designing my first ever scrap book. In fact, I'm going to stop writing right now to get back to it. I've already taken a photo of Matilda, which she didn't really like, but she was the most convenient model at the time. I have SO much to record just from this year!

Thank you, Abby, for being there for me and for sharing this very special day with me,

Abigail Van Buren Masterson

April 16

Dear Abby,

Pap surprised me when he came home early from the diner and found me practicing the piano. He wanted to know why he had never heard me play before, but nodded as if he understood when I told him that I did not like to play when people were around. We've never lived in one place long enough for me to experience a recital or playing in public. Since Mom has been my sole teacher, there has been no opportunity. This summer, though, both Joey and I are enrolling in piano lessons at the college so I will have to get used to an audience. It just makes me really uncomfortable, though.

Joey, on the other hand, can't wait to show off his talents. What a ham! Mom has often said that if we combined Joey's confidence and my ability we would have a star.

Before Pap left to return to the diner and leave me to practice in private, he showed me the little closet where Grandmother kept a rather impressive collection of sheet music and piano books. I would not want for music for a long, long time. Every piano lesson book used by Mom, Aunt Katie and even my uncles was organized by date and difficulty level in Grandmother's beautiful calligraphy. I wish I had known her when she was still healthy and living at home. I bet she was a real classy lady.

Sincerely,
Abigail Van Buren Masterson

April 18

Dear Abby,

Mom, Katie, Miss Hendershot and I went to the first MS Support Meeting since Nora passed away. I anticipated a lot of tears and emotions, but did NOT expect the large number of people who came to pay their respects to someone who evidently was a remarkable lady.

Miss Hendershot gave a tribute to her friend, and thanked all of the group members for their uninterrupted support. I guess Miss Hendershot used to bring Nora to all of the meetings until the trip became too cumbersome for them both. The MS group visited them instead and that is why the group only met once a month at the YWCA. They decided to better spend their time on the other weeks to visit home- riddened MS victims. I don't know why, but that really brought tears to my eyes as well as everyone else's.

There was a picture of Nora on the refreshment table and I know that photo will haunt me for a very long time. She was a very beautiful woman with long dark hair and bright blue, smiling eyes. She looked SO young and so VERY NOT deserving of such a crippling disease. My breath kinda got stuck in my chest for what seemed like an hour before I could release it and continue breathing normally. I know now that I really, truly will devote my research project to MS, in honor of my mother and of Nora, and all of the other undeserving recipients of this disease.

I am glad that I went to the meeting this evening. This personal side of MS is one that is not acknowledged by doctors, drug manufactures and researcher. THIS is what living with MS is all about.

Linda announced that the group will now meet semi-monthly and she asked for names of anyone who requires a home visit.

I think that we will definitely be coming back. In fact, I think Mom, Aunt Katie and Miss Hendershot are going to be quite active in the group. I would also like to play an active part if I am allowed. This is really an incredible group of people.

I am humbled,
Abigail Van Buren Masterson

April 20

Dear Abby,

Patti and I decided to put my new birthday camera to use by taking some personal photos and pictures of the neighborhood to send to our pen pals. She knows how to download my camera contents onto the computer and print our pictures from there, so we both will have a real nice letter to send before school on Monday.

I STILL have not written to Sheila's old pen pal because Lisette has opened a door for me that I cannot ignore. She writes to me every week, and I'm really curious about how she keeps this up writing to two different people AND completing school work AND entertaining her many boyfriends AND finding time to eat and sleep. She has never once mentioned Sheila but according to Sheila, her new pen pal writes QUITE extensive letters, describing the exciting life she lives in Paris. I am more than a little confused. I'm not going to give Sheila the satisfaction of knowing my confusion, though. I kinda smell something a little "fishy" about the whole situation, but that's me being judgmental again.

Anyway, I am enjoying my new camera and can't wait to take it to the nursing home on Sunday to take some pictures of Grandmother and me.

Your friend the Shutterbug,
Abigail Van Buren Masterson

April 28

Dear Abby,

I am definitely regretting insisting that Mom participate in Yoga. No, erase that. I DEFINITELY regret agreeing to JOIN Mom in her participation in Yoga.

It's A LOT harder than it sounds.

Yoga brings to my mind soft music, peaceful waterfalls, gentle breathing and a spiritual experience. Wrong!

Yoga hurts!

My legs are on fire, my back feels strangely twisted and my mind is NOT at peace.

Mom struggled at first, too, but finally "embraced" the experience and said that she can over look the immediate physical discomfort for the promise of the "potential results".

I think there is something wrong with me. I mean, I'm only 13 years old and relatively healthy. Mom is nearly 30 years old, the mother of two children, and has multiple sclerosis. I guess all of those vitamins and natural remedies have buffed up her immunity to muscle stress related PAIN of this incredibly ridiculous and unnatural practice of twisting one's body into inhuman positions! Geesh! I'M NOT A PRETZEL!

I know I promised her that I would do this with her and I have been fairly faithful in practicing with her every night, even if it is just for a few minutes. I really thought she would give it up after those first attempts when she, too, felt frustrated with the whole thing.

Well, Mother Dearest has proven to me, once again, that she is determined to not allow MS rule her life and to beat the crap out of Yoga while she's at it.

I don't even have the strength to "Om", so I'll just say goodnight.

Abigail Van Buren Masterson

May 5

Dear Abby,

A draw back from being enrolled in an eighth grade class as a seventh grader is that sometimes we are not "on the same page". Today Miss Tortellini asked the class to write an essay (in English) that describes their feelings about leaving junior high to become a high school freshman. I could have completed that assignment (and probably in French because it would be very short) by saying "I just want to survive the eighth grade!"

I am happy that I will have practically the same teachers next year. There is something comforting about knowing who my teachers will be and already having a relationship (good or bad) with them. When Miss Hendershot asked me earlier in the year if she could possibly read my journal at the end of the school, I was nervous about that, but a lot has happened between then and now, and I don't mind at all. I've never felt so comfortable with anyone, let alone a teacher. Miss Hendershot has become quite a surprise. She's a great teacher, but quiet and not real dynamic like Miss Tortellini; yet she's a REAL person underneath the teacher uniform. She really seems to understand what her students are thinking. I hate that it has taken the death of her dear friend for her to open up so much to us. At least I think that is why she has changed. I suppose the stress of caring for Nora really aged her attitude for a while. She even dresses younger these days and isn't as homely as I once thought.

I don't really know "why" she's so interested in my journal, but I'll hand it over to her at the end of the school year. There are only a few empty pages left and I plan to ask Mom for a new one soon. Miss Hendershot said that I could tear out any pages that I felt were too confidential to share, but after looking through it, I don't see much that I can't trust her with. My little comments about Head Cheerleader Sheila might be a bit incriminating, but I think I can trust the teacher/student oath that teachers sign upon college graduation. (Teachers DO have such things, don't they?)

I cannot believe that this school year is almost over! There are just two more weeks until final exams!

Oh, by the way, I don't think that Lisette is actually writing to Sheila. We exchanged email addresses (Mom allowed me to have one of my own when Lisette sent me hers. I guess she sees it as educational.) and we have been corresponding some that way, even though we both decided that getting snail mail is more exciting.

Anyway, emailing has really brought us closer and I feel like I'm really getting to know her. I don't think that first letter from her was a true representation of who she is. In fact, I'm beginning to believe that we are more alike than I would have ever believed. When I asked in French class if anyone else was e-mailing, only one other person commented. And that person was NOT Sheila. In fact, she said that her pen pal does not have a computer!

I don't know what to think, Abby. I don't want to accuse Sheila of lying but after all she has done to me, the satisfaction of seeing her squirm would be tres sensationnel!

Trying not to be judgmental (again),
Abigail Van Buren Masterson

May 6

Dear Abby,

When I got home from school today, Matilda was sitting nervously on my bed wearing Joey's eye glasses while he explained to her the importance of a balanced diet. She did NOT look happy, but I guess her curiosity kept her somewhat interested. She did paw toward me to indicate that I should not (or most definitely SHOULD) interrupt, but he calmly placed a little hand on her head (I think she's getting used to being his puppet) and continued his speech.

He later explained that she was his needed audience to practice his presentation for school. When I asked him about the eyeglasses, he looked at me like I was the crazy one. He said he had to "get into character" and that his teacher wore glasses so he had to make Matilda look like his teacher, Mrs. Veltri.

I don't recall Mrs. Veltri sporting whiskers, but I didn't argue.

Joey sure can be weird sometimes, but he really is serious about his school work.

I had difficulty concentrating on my own homework after that, though. Every time I looked at Matilda, I saw Mr. Davis with a tail and black ears. I don't think I'll do so well on my social studies exam tomorrow (thank goodness it's just a practice final).

Meow,
Abigail Van Buren Masterson

May 7

Dear Abby,

I knew it, I knew it, I knew it!

Sheila has only written one letter to Lisette and Lisette wrote back to tell her that she was "pleased as punch" (or some French phrase equivalent) with her current pen pal and could not possibly afford the time from her school work to write to two people. I do not know why Sheila felt it necessary to lie about her correspondence, but Lisette spilled the beans in our weekly e-mail last night. I guess Sheila took the opportunity to "malign" Abigail Van Buren Masterson in her one and only letter to France, and Lisette took offense to the negative remarks about me. ESPECIALLY since Sheila felt it necessary to "put down" seventh graders, not realizing that Lisette, too, is a SEVENTH GRADER. Oh, Abby, I do not like my wicked pleasure in knowing of Sheila's disgraceful behavior, but I sure am enjoying it.

What do I do about it, though? Put on your Advice Hat, Abby. Do I say anything to Sheila? To Miss Tortellini? To the Cheerleader Clones? Do I retaliate at all or do I remain demurely silent?

Your servant,
Abigail Van Buren Masterson

May 14

Dear Abby,

Guess what?

I didn't have to say a word to anybody about Sheila's indiscretion. She told on herself. Today when we gave our final report on our pen pal experience, she reported that she and her French pal had parted ways due to incompatibility. What a loser! Why couldn't she just say that she messed up? She looked right at me when she told the class that it was impossible to converse sensibly with an immature SEVENTH GRADER and that she would request an older pen pal in the future. Good grief!

Miss Tortelllini looked a bit miffed at first, but when Sheila wasn't looking, she rolled her eyes and called on the next volunteer. The Cheerleader Clones saw Miss Tortellini's reaction, though, and really ticked off their fearless leader when they refused to tell her why they were snickering. Oh, how sweet the sounds of revenge! And I didn't have to do a thing.

Thank you, Abby, for your reply to my request for advice,
Abigail Van Buren Masterson

P.S. I think Lisette and I are going to get along just fine.

May 27

Dear Abby,

Wow and viola! (I have given up on finding a new "catch phrase". I like this one just fine and I don't really care any more if it is not completely correct. Maybe I'll find a new one next year.) Final exams are OVER! I am one short step away from being an eighth grader and "finis" with the seventh grade.

Most of the students are celebrating the end to this school year, but, honestly, I'm a bit sad, Abby. I have had an absolutely AWESOME year. Even with the negatives like Mom's multiple sclerosis and issues with Head Cheerleader Sheila, this year has given me so many blessings. I found my grandparents and am living in a beautiful house and am surrounded by family. Mom has found a "place" with Aunt Katie and Miss Hendershot in the MS Support group and she is seriously considering working full time for the National MS Society (from home on the computer, of course, because there is NO WAY she is moving somewhere else now that she's home).

Summer looms ahead and I CANNOT wait to see what it has in store for us.

I've already promised Joey that we will clean up the tree house and spend some time up there (even if I really am a little scared of heights). Patti is going away to church camp for two weeks and wants me to go with her, but I selfishly just want to enjoy my new home. I'm surprised that Mom agrees with me on this. I figured she would want to "walk down memory lane" by encouraging me to experience some of her childhood activities. I think she is also being selfish because she wants to visit Grandmother a lot more and doesn't want to go alone. I'll gladly be her scapegoat if it will bring her and her mother closer together.

Lisette and I are planning to join an internet book club and I'm looking forward to that. She's a lot more studious than I first thought, and she does NOT have a string of boyfriends like she originally led me to believe. She admitted that she was trying to impress me at first and realized how silly she sounded after reading Sheila's letter to her. She does take ballet lessons, but she's only ridden a horse one time and she's terrified of the water, so the Olympics are out of the question. I'm glad she trusted me enough to admit these things and I'm even gladder that Sheila isn't her cup of tea. I think it would be really exciting to actually visit her in France sometime, but airplane rides are not high on my "to do" list, so I'll just postpone travel plans for a while.

Joey and I also have our piano lessons to think about. I think it will be fun to take lessons from someone besides Mom, but I'm still a little nervous about playing in front of a stranger. Pap says he will be my silent audience any time I need him.

I only got a "B" on my research project, but I'm still proud of what I learned in the process. Miss Hendershot thought it was a fine effort and commended me on tackling such a personal topic. She recommended that I keep a copy of the paper filed away for future use, though. With some "polish" she said it would be an impressive "missive" for a possible high school project. (She really loves her vocabulary, even if it does wear out the listener.

I've spent a lot of time looking up words that she throws out. My dictionary got a lot of use this year.)

Adam has promised to take me to the community swimming pool and hang out with me on the days that he doesn't have football practice. He actually was invited to try out for the high school junior varsity team! He's really excited and I am very proud of him.

Joey is ready for summer, too, I think. He's not quite as sentimental about the end of the school year as I am. In fact, he's decided that he wants to go to college with Mom if she decides to go. He thinks he's ready and doesn't need to continue his public education. Patti just rolls her eyes at his attitude, but I'm beginning to think that he might actually be a child prodigy of some kind. He certainly helped me pass my math class!

Well, tomorrow is our official "last day" and I need to get ready before going to bed. Patti and I are wearing our red, white and blue shorts outfits in honor of the upcoming Memorial Day weekend as well as our last public appearance together at MJHS.

It's been fun, Abby. Thanks for listening.

Your friend,
Abigail Van Buren Masterson

June 21

Dear Abby,

A true teacher is one who cares for the needs and concerns of every student, and not just academics. I believe I had the honor of being in the presence of a "true teacher" this year.

Miss Hendershot returned my journal to my house today with a VERY special surprise for me. When she realized that my personal journal was also an extended letter to you, she wrote to you (via your daughter since you are no longer in the advice business that you handed over to her) and she got a response.

Addressed to me.

From Dear Abby.

And here it is:

Dear Abigail Van Buren Masterson,

I am so honored to be the target of your many thoughts and memories. I, too, think it is extremely interesting and unusual for two Abigail Van Buren's to exist in this world.

Your interest in my life is quite flattering. Even though your research has taken a new direction, I am glad that I had a hand in your decision to research a topic of much greater importance. I suppose this is an indication of my life's work. I have guided a young mind.

Good luck with your life's endeavors.

In bond,

Abby

Je suis Abigail

I cannot believe that Miss Hendershot did this for me and I cannot believe that you actually WROTE BACK.

Miss Hendershot did not have to do this and neither did you! You both went out of your way to touch a student. I am more than touched. I am speechless.

Miss Hendershot is a true teacher.

And so are you Dear Abby.

Sincerely,
Abigail Van Buren Masterson
And I, too, am Abigail.